PRAISE FOR LAUREN LAYNE

"Exemplary contemporary romance."

—*Library Journal*

"Flawless contemporary romance—witty, sexy, heartfelt, and hugely entertaining."

—*USA TODAY*

Yours in Scandal

Yours in Scandal

LAUREN LAYNE

 Montlake

Text copyright © 2020 by Lauren Layne
All rights reserved.

Published by Montlake, Seattle

www.apub.com

Amazon, the Amazon logo, and Montlake are trademarks of Amazon.com, Inc., or its affiliates.

ISBN-13: 9781542018807
ISBN-10: 1542018803

Cover design by Letitia Hasser

Cover photography by Wander Aguiar Photography

Printed in the United States of America

Yours in Scandal

Chapter One

"So. How does it feel to be listed in the same company as Brad Pitt, George Clooney, and Hugh Jackman?"

Robert Davenport didn't bother to look up from the police commissioner's report he was reviewing as he answered. "Utterly absurd. Actually, no. Make that painfully ridiculous."

"Come on. You're not flattered? Your Hollywood good looks are finally getting the attention they deserve," the other man said, dropping into the chair opposite Robert's desk.

Robert very slowly, very subtly let out an exhale of irritation and, after taking his time putting the report away, gave his campaign manager his full attention. "Why would that be flattering? Unlike the aforementioned, I'm *not* Hollywood. I spend my days trying to make the country's largest city a better, safer place, not shooting a fake gun in front of a green screen."

"Well, lucky for us, all your do-gooder integrity has made you the hottest thing on the newsstand these days," Martin said, tossing the magazine onto Robert's desk and leaning back, hands behind his head.

Robert picked up the magazine and dropped it in the trash without a single glance at the cover. The image of his face on the front of *Citizen* alongside the aggrandized Man of the Year! headline had been shoved at him by every person he knew since its publication last week.

Undeterred by Robert's indifference, Martin tipped forward again, letting the wooden legs of the fussy chair thud heavily against the rug. "Come on, Robbie. It's gold. Pure fucking gold."

"It's shit," Robert countered. "Pure shit. Also, did we have an appointment?"

The question was rhetorical. Martin was most definitely not on his calendar, and in a career that lent itself to very little downtime, Robert hated unnecessary interruptions. Something his longtime campaign manager knew full well.

"Your face is in every grocery store and Walmart in America," Martin pointed out. "If I didn't stop by to tell you to take advantage of the moment, you should fire my ass."

The last statement was uttered in the arrogant tone of a man completely confident in his job security, and Robert tried not to chafe at his campaign manager's assumptions. Martin had been in the political arena since Robert was a boy—specifically, Martin had been in the *Davenport* political arena. He'd worked for Robert's father before the man's untimely death, which, according to Martin, made him "practically family."

"You got my strategy emails on how to capitalize on the magazine cover?" Martin asked.

"Got them. Deleted them," Robert said.

Martin's impatience was plain. "This is free publicity, Robbie. The type of publicity that makes you a household name. And you know where being a household name gets you? The White House."

Robert leaned back in his chair and gave in to the urge to crack his knuckles. It was a habit he'd mostly kicked in college, but the compulsion still came back to him when he was feeling particularly frustrated or pissed off. Today, he was feeling both.

Robert nodded in the direction of the magazine in the trash can. "Did you read it?"

"Of course I've read it. I had the team grab the best pull quotes to start brainstorming how to work them into TV spots." Martin paused. "Have *you* read it?"

"I read the cover. The headline pretty much says it all," Robert grumbled.

"Hell yes it does," Martin said enthusiastically. He leaned down and lifted his old-school briefcase onto the desk and opened it.

Martin pulled out another copy of the magazine, and as tempted as Robert was to trash that one as well, he knew it was futile. Martin would keep them coming until he'd said his piece.

The campaign manager pointed at the cover, his finger tapping on each damning word as he read the headline aloud. "Man of the Year: Robert Davenport. Powerful. Charming. Single?"

Robert winced but stayed silent.

"The question mark is good," Martin continued. "Single. Question mark."

"How is that good? If they'd done their homework, they'd have known it was Single, *Period*."

"Be glad they didn't."

Robert gave Martin a wary glance. "Do I even want to know?"

Martin leaned back, folding his hands over the bulge of his stomach. When Martin had joined Robert's father's campaign team nearly thirty years ago, he'd been a wiry, ambitious twentysomething eager to claim his place in history as part of the Davenport legacy. He'd done exactly that, though with Robert Jr. instead of Sr., as he'd originally planned. Martin had been Robert's campaign manager since the very beginning. He was no longer twentysomething. His lanky frame had thickened into middle-aged paunch. His ambition, however, had remained.

No, his ambition had *increased*.

Robert felt disloyal for thinking it, but he'd worried for some time now that Martin's ambition had been replaced by something a bit more sordid. He wouldn't go so far as to say his campaign manager played dirty. But there was a cynicism and derision to the way Martin talked about the very people they were trying to serve, and Robert had the nagging sense that Martin cared about winning more than he did their *reasons* for winning. More and more frequently Robert concluded his meetings with Martin with a sense of unease in his stomach. But Martin was one of the last remaining links he had to his father, and for that, he could tolerate quite a lot.

"Look, Robbie . . ."

Robert stifled a sigh. *Here we go.*

"Charm is what got you elected as New York City's youngest mayor. It's also what's made you almost nauseatingly popular over the past eight years. But you're not a novelty anymore."

"Is this supposed to be a pep talk?" Robert asked.

"That's Kenny's job," Martin said with a wave of his hand, then frowned. "Where is that boy, anyway? Why's he not lurking in the corner like usual?"

Referring to thirty-seven-year-old Kenny Lamb as a boy was one of Martin's favorite ways of undermining Robert's chief of staff.

"Honeymoon," Robert said, with no small amount of regret. Kenny was a master of getting Robert out of conversations like this one, but he'd had to make do without his right-hand man the past couple of weeks, and he was starting to feel the strain. Kenny wouldn't have been able to stop the whole Man of the Year debacle, but he'd at least have been able to run interference and ensure the damn magazine wasn't shoved in Robert's face ten times a day.

"Oh, right. What was I saying?" Martin asked.

"That I'm a washed-up has-been," Robert prompted wryly.

To Martin's point, elected at age twenty-seven, Robert had indeed been the youngest mayor in New York City's history, and come January when his successor took over, he would be one of the youngest *ex-mayors* in New York City history at thirty-five.

But despite Martin's dire tone, Robert was plenty young by politician standards. Still, that didn't make it any easier to say goodbye to what he had come to think of as the best damn job in the world. He'd been born and raised in this city, and serving as its mayor for two terms had been an honor.

He'd like to think the city would agree with him. Robert had every reason to believe that he would be elected for a third term, if it weren't for the two-term limit. But one didn't survive in a place like New York City, much less the world of politics, by living in the past. In order to thrive, it wasn't about the present—it was all about the future. What was *next*.

As grating as Martin could be when he stopped by without a heads-up, Robert knew his campaign manager understood this fact better than anyone. In fact, Martin's entire job was to focus on the future of Robert's career, and it was a job he was good at. Robert might consider himself a damn good mayor, just as he'd been a stellar city councilman before that, but it had taken someone with know-how to get an early-twenties kid in the door, and to Martin's credit, he'd done exactly that.

"I didn't say you were washed up," Martin said, giving the magazine another flick. "Quite the opposite. You know what I see when I look at this face? The face of a governor. That's who."

"You're getting ahead of yourself."

"Which is exactly what you pay me to do," Martin pointed out. "I understand you've wanted to limit campaign efforts while you're still in the mayor's seat, but in a few months, someone else will be sitting in that very chair, and we'll be on a dangerously short timeline to make a bid for gov."

Robert nodded. "I'm aware. But I've been clear on this. I don't believe in multitasking, not in my line of work. I'll start being an aspiring governor when the next mayor is sworn in in January. Not a day before."

Martin leaned forward. "I'm not asking you to jump with both feet into the governor's race, just . . . dip a toe in. Don't let this"—he nudged the magazine—"go to waste."

It was on the tip of Robert's tongue to protest. He knew campaigning was a part of the job—sometimes it felt like it *was* the job. But he'd always stood his ground about his priority being the job he had, not the one he hoped to have a year from now.

And yet, he wasn't an idiot. He knew that as obnoxious and embarrassing as it was to be titled Man of the Year, a moniker usually reserved for stars of the latest Hollywood blockbuster or Oscar bait, it was also every politician's wet dream. You couldn't buy this kind of national publicity, and he'd had it dropped in his lap.

Martin was right—he'd be a fool to waste it.

Powerful. Charming. Single?

He didn't mind the first two. Being perceived as powerful was a boon in politics. He'd spent most of his life carefully cultivating the charming part, and he'd like to think it came from a place of authenticity.

The *single* delineation, though. That just straight up pissed him off.

Robert gave Martin a cautious look. "Explain to me why my relationship status is relevant."

"A single, twentysomething mayor-elect is a bachelor. A single, midthirties ex-mayor is just sad."

Robert made an exaggerated grunting noise. "Ouch."

Martin continued, showing no mercy. "We've already run focus groups on people's reception to the *Citizen* cover. Generally positive. You're hot, no surprise there. But ask 'em how they'd feel about a single, thirtysomething guy as a governor? Or in Washington? They hesitate. And when pressed for comment, the overwhelming consensus is 'it's a little weird.'"

Robert itched to crack his knuckles, but he bit the inside of his cheek instead.

The commentary about his single status wasn't new. And he knew Martin was right. When he'd been elected at twenty-seven, his youth and unmarried status had been a novelty. *Charming.*

At thirty-five, without so much as a hint of a girlfriend on the horizon, the situation seemed to escalate with every interview. The public appearances were even worse. He couldn't show his face at a fund-raiser or gala without an overt come-on from nearly every single woman in the place, from recent college graduates all the way up to silver-haired divorcées. Silver foxettes, Kenny called them.

It had gotten so bad he could no longer tell which ones had First Lady aspirations, and which were simply looking for bragging rights of having flirted with him. He even got the sense some of the married ones hoped to lure him into impropriety.

They could try all they wanted. Robert had been careful to avoid even a trace of misconduct his entire adult life, and he had no intention of letting any woman, of any age group, drag him into scandal now.

Unfortunately, these days he was feeling like he was stuck in a *damned if you do, damned if you don't* situation. Apparently, there was such a thing as too much avoidance of romantic entanglements. Still, he refused to believe that he lived in a world where he'd be denied a job he was qualified for—a job he was good at—simply because he hadn't put a ring on a woman's finger.

Robert threw out his usual argument. "Plenty of mayors, New York and otherwise, have been unmarried at the time of their tenure. Hell, most of them had downright messy personal relations."

"But they did *have* personal relations," Martin said. "Face it, man, puritan as voters can be, the tide is turning. Happily married is still the preferred status, but barring that, they'll take a playboy over a monk."

"I'm not a monk," Robert snapped, even though the number of nights he'd gone to bed alone in the last eight years belied that. It wasn't that he didn't enjoy women. He just hadn't met one he enjoyed half as much as he did his job. And as far as the physical matters went, finding a woman he was attracted to *and* whom he trusted to be discreet was no easy task.

"No, you're not," Martin said, "which is a perfect segue to the reason I'm here . . ."

Robert lifted his hand to his forehead and tried not to feel frustrated by the fact that Martin was forever working an angle. Realistically, he knew he needed someone like Martin in his camp. But if he was completely honest with himself, it was harder and harder to like the man. Harder still to get on board with Martin's various schemes.

"You've got two minutes," Robert said tiredly.

"All I need," Martin said, already reaching into his open briefcase and pulling out two tablets.

Robert lifted his eyebrows. "You carry two iPads?" The fiftysomething man was usually a little more analog.

"Caroline told me to get with the times," he said, referring to his college-age daughter. "Okay, here we go. We're making the play for governor next year, and we've got a damn good shot. Your approval ratings are high, your celeb status is through the roof thanks to the magazine, but we've got two obstacles. Big ones. First . . ." He handed Robert one of the tablets, and Robert was unsurprised to see a photo of the current governor on the screen.

Robert lowered the iPad and glared at Martin in exasperation. "Believe it or not, I don't need to pay you to know that the popular two-time incumbent has already announced he's going for a third term. And by the way, George Brennan's bachelor status hasn't seemed to hurt him."

"George Brennan is a widower, not a bachelor," Martin said. "Crucial difference, and another excellent segue."

"To what?"

Martin gave a slow, smug smile as he took the iPad back. "The rumors."

Robert didn't need to ask which rumors. George Brennan was about as close to a stock character in a political melodrama as you could get. Good-looking for nearing sixty. Personable, well spoken, distinguished.

Officially, the man hadn't made a single misstep. *Unofficially*, rumors had been swirling for years, everything from recreational drug use to paid escort services to a vile temper. But come election time, the rumors stayed rumors, and the man remained untouchable.

Well, nearly untouchable. Martin handed Robert the iPad once more, this time with a different but equally recognizable face—at least to anyone in New York politics.

Robert looked down at the laughing twentysomething girl at a party, the iconic red keg cup in hand, long blonde hair spilling down her slim back as she laughed. At first glance, she seemed a gorgeous young thing having the time of her life. At second glance, he registered the way she was looking straight at the camera, a touch of defiance in her blue eyes.

George Brennan may not have made many missteps, at least publicly, but his daughter had made plenty. In the age-old story of rebellious children, Addie Brennan had been the governor's Achilles' heel in the last election—wild and unpredictable. There'd been a litany of drug charges, topless photos, and hanging out with a crowd *very* different from her father's.

Still, it was old news. Brennan had distanced himself from his daughter and won the election, and Robert hadn't so much as heard her name in years.

"This is your plan?" he asked skeptically. "Pulling up five-year-old gossip of the man's daughter?"

Martin merely handed Robert the second iPad.

He accepted it, studied the image that was displayed for a moment, then looked up at his campaign manager, more confused than ever. "I'm not following."

"Look again."

Impatient, Robert glanced down at the woman on the second iPad: a brunette in glasses, with a librarian bun, on her laptop at a coffee shop. Robert didn't recognize her, and he couldn't think what she had to do with George Brennan. Or Addie Brennan, he thought, looking back at the blonde girl.

Unless . . .

His eyes flicked between the two iPads. He could think of only one reason Martin would be showing him pictures of two very different women.

Because they *weren't* different women.

"Holy shit," Robert murmured, squinting and sort of seeing similarities in the face shape, but he really had to be looking for them. The brunette was attractive, certainly, but not in the flashy *look at me!* way of her younger, blonde self.

"Yup," Martin said smugly. "She goes by Adeline Blake now. Dropped the Brennan altogether, and took her middle name as her last."

"Where the hell has she been? Hiding in plain sight this whole time?"

Martin shook his head. "As far as I can tell, Adeline Blake didn't exist until about a year ago. Where Addie Brennan was hiding the few years before that, I don't have a clue. Yet."

Robert handed back both tablets. "The Clark Kent transformation is interesting, but I don't see what it has to do with Brennan. He hasn't mentioned his daughter in years, and by the looks of it, she's after an entirely fresh start. I'm not going to dig up her old scandals."

"Not her scandals, no," Martin said. "Even if we wanted to, it's old news. All but the tawdriest tabloids would see right through us."

"Then what's your plan?" Robert asked warily, instinctively knowing Martin had one brewing.

"You and I both know that Brennan's not half as clean as he looks, but he's got an A-plus cleanup crew. Not a single whisper about the hookers or the heroin has made it to mainstream media. Somehow, the man's managed to maintain the loyalty of everyone around him, either by bribery, blackmail, or just good old-fashioned ass-kissing."

"Hardly the first politician to do so."

Martin lifted his eyebrows. "The Boy Scout sounds almost cynical."

Robert narrowed his eyes in warning. He tolerated Martin calling him Robbie, as his father had done. But he hated when the press referred to him as a Boy Scout, and Martin knew it.

"Anyway," Martin muttered, averting his eyes from Robert's glare. "If we're going to get dirt on him, we've got to get as close to the source as possible. And who's closer than his daughter?"

"By all accounts, just about anyone. He basically disowned her, and she changed her name. I think it's safe to say they're estranged."

"Exactly. I'm guessing daughter is none too fond of daddy dearest. And I'm guessing she's witnessed some serious shit." He looked at Robert expectantly.

Robert shook his head. "I will not destroy a woman's life to get an edge in a campaign against her father."

"Jesus, Davenport, nobody's suggesting you ruin her life. It's just some good old-fashioned research on the opposition."

"I won't play dirty."

Martin held up his hands. "Mud won't get anywhere near you. I'm not suggesting you sell her out. You don't even have to tell her you know who she is. But it can't hurt to open up the channels of communication. Who knows what she might confide to the very single Man of the Year?"

Robert shook his head more emphatically this time. "Unequivocally no. When I said I wasn't a monk, I didn't mean I'd stoop to seducing a woman to fuel your smear campaign."

"Calm down, Boy Scout—nobody said anything about seduction."

"Then what, I'm just supposed to bump into her at Starbucks and wait for her to tell me what kind of shady shit her father's into?"

"Give me some credit, Robbie. The woman runs a premier event planning company here in the city."

"And?"

"And you like to entertain. You mentioned throwing a last hurrah here at Gracie Mansion in a few weeks, did you not?"

"Yes, but—"

"And Jada just had twins, so you're short a party planner."

Damn. That much was true. His longtime event planner *had* just given birth to twins, and he *had* been meaning to ask his assistant where they were on finding a stand-in. But it wasn't going to be Governor Brennan's wild child daughter who, from the looks of it, wanted nothing to do with politics. He wanted the governor's seat, but not if he had to step on someone else to get there. Robert would get there on his own merit, or not at all.

"We can beat Brennan without bringing his daughter into it," Robert said.

Martin lifted an eyebrow. "Can we? He's got the incumbent advantage. Your approval ratings are good, but so are the governor's."

Robert blew out a breath. "How can that be? The man's an egotistical poser."

"Behind closed doors, yes. On camera, he comes across as a goddamn Founding Father."

Robert gave in to the urge to crack his knuckles again, hating that Martin was right. He believed down to his very soul that he was the better man for the job. He and the governor had worked together for years, and while Robert knew that playing nice with people you didn't agree with was half the battle in politics, his dislike of the governor went beyond any policy differences. There was a slick smugness to the man, and Robert's gut told him the whispers of corruption weren't off base.

Knowing it was one thing. Proving that the governor was unscrupulous was something else entirely. The man was too careful, and no one person ever spent enough time in his orbit to learn all his skeletons.

No one except his daughter.

For a fleeting moment, Robert considered Martin's suggestion. If anyone had proof of the governor's lack of principles, it was someone who'd lived with him for decades.

Robert shoved the thought aside. She had distanced herself from her father for a reason. He would respect that. "I won't drag Brennan's daughter into something she wants no part of."

Martin shrugged as he stood. "So find out if she wants to be a part of it. She'll be here tomorrow at two p.m. to talk about your party."

Chapter Two

Adeline Blake had thought she'd learned to control the troublesome urges of her youth as Addie Brennan. *Control.* But not abandon altogether.

She still liked to dance, but in the privacy of her apartment, not on top of bars.

She still liked tequila, but in a civilized, sipping manner, body shots a thing of the past.

She still wore sexy underwear, but she no longer showed it to strangers, and she definitely didn't take it *off* for strangers.

If she swore, it was under her breath; if she yelled, it was into a pillow; and while she still loved the thrill of adventure, her new definition of living on the edge was trying to catch a cab on a rainy Friday afternoon when already running late for an appointment.

Things she did *not* do: go anywhere near the world of politics or put herself in the presence of anyone who stood a better-than-average chance of recognizing her as Addie Brennan. Which did not explain what she was doing outside Gracie Mansion in Yorkville, mentally gearing up for a meeting with the mayor of New York City.

Who, according to every newsstand in the city, was the sexiest man alive, or the universe's hottest bachelor, or some dubious honor awarded to men with great jawlines and massive egos.

Who, according to the email she'd received requesting a consultation, was in need of a last-minute event planner. That an invitation for such a high-profile client had come to Adeline Blake of Jet Set Events was flattering. That it had simultaneously come from the mayor's office to Addie Brennan was a red flag. Especially if the rumors about him making a bid for the governor's seat next year were true.

Which led her to the last of those pesky bad qualities that she hadn't apparently shaken by age twenty-eight: curiosity.

When the man who may or may not be trying to oust your bastard father from office summoned you, you said *maybe*.

When the mayor of New York City and oft-theorized future president of the United States summoned you as his potential party planner, you said *perhaps*.

And when the Man of the Year summoned you as a *woman* . . . you said *yes*.

Which is where the curiosity came in. Addie was dying to see if he was as hot in person as he was in photos and on TV.

Adeline never claimed to be a saint. Just a *slightly* reformed sinner.

She gave a quick glance down at her appearance to make sure she looked the part of a Manhattan professional.

Tailored black slacks, *check*. Fitted blouse with an appropriate two buttons undone, *check*. Black blazer to ensure red bra under the white shirt wasn't visible, *check*. Black pumps just high enough to be stylish, but not so high as to be absurd, *check*. Deep side part of her hair smooth, bun firmly in place at the nape of her neck, *check*.

She smiled. Even without her glasses as an extra layer of disguise, she was fully confident that the mayor would see exactly what she wanted him to see: Adeline Blake, premier event planner.

All vestiges of Addie were safely tucked away.

Cool smile firmly in place, Adeline entered the mansion. One of the mayor's assistants had emailed her the process for getting to his offices, so she was prepared for the bag check and the scrutiny of her identification.

She swallowed, unexpected nervousness rushing through her. Gracie Mansion wasn't exactly like the Executive Mansion in Albany, but it was close enough to flood her with memories, none of them pleasant.

Addie, how many times have I told you not to run? Addie, stop that. Quiet, Addie, I can't concentrate. Damn it, Addie, I'm busy. What the hell are you wearing, young lady?

Shoving the toxic thoughts aside, she fixed her professional smile on the middle-aged assistant who greeted her. "Hi, I'm Adeline Blake, here to see Mayor Davenport. I'm a little early."

"No worries," the woman said with a friendly smile. "His one-thirty had to reschedule. Let me see if he's available to meet with you now. Have a seat, and I'll be right back."

Adeline did as she was told.

A moment later the woman returned and gestured her forward. "He said to head on in. End of the hall," she said, pointing.

Adeline thanked her and walked in the direction indicated, assuaging her curiosity by taking in every detail. She was uncomfortably acquainted with New York state politics, but New York *City* was a whole other ball game. Something she'd enjoyed reminding her father of, after she'd identified it as one of his hot buttons.

George Brennan had never made peace with the fact that he lived in the one state where the mayor of a single city continually overshadowed the governor of the entire state. And that had been *before* Robert Davenport was named Man of the Year, launching his celebrity status to a borderline nightmare level.

The door was open, and Adeline rapped a knuckle against the doorjamb. "Mayor Davenport?"

He was studying a folder on his desk, but his head snapped up at the interruption, his gaze colliding with hers.

Adeline sucked in a breath.

Well, that answers that question. He is definitely *as hot in person.*

She should have been prepared. The man's face was everywhere, after all. She'd known he had sandy-brown hair, hazel eyes, and a classically handsome face that the camera loved.

But the cameras had missed plenty.

The pictures didn't quite capture the gold flecks in his eyes, or the raw masculinity emanating off him in waves. Nor did photos catch that the polished politician's smile currently spreading across his face, while perfectly friendly and authentic, she suspected also served as an armor of sorts.

Instinct told her that what you saw was what you got with Mayor Davenport, but there was plenty he'd never let you see.

"Ms. Blake?" he said, rising and extending a hand.

"Yes. A pleasure, Mr. Mayor," she said, sending a rare silent thank-you to her past for teaching protocol for addressing public officials. Mr. Mayor. Mayor Davenport. Sir.

In her teens, she'd added more mocking salutations to the mix when addressing her father. *Your Majesty. Your Highness. Your Excellence.*

She spared the mayor her derision. For now.

His fingers were dry and firm as they closed over hers, shaking her hand with confidence befitting a man who'd probably shaken thousands of hands over the course of his career. Then his gaze locked on hers, his eyes seeming to glow wolf's gold, in a way that felt anything but routine.

Her stomach flipped. Irritated with herself, she tugged her hand away.

His assessing look transformed back to charming politician, and he gestured for her to sit in the chair opposite his. "So, you're an event planner."

"I am." She sat, setting her purse on the chair beside her. "And if I may say so, sir, I'm a bit surprised to be meeting with you in person."

"Why's that?"

She'd forgotten this, the way good politicians knew to ask more questions than they answered. "I would have thought the mayor of New York City would delegate party planning to an assistant."

"True. And Darlene is more than capable of handling it," he said with a slight smile. "But I'm not a CEO hosting a gathering on behalf of the city. I'm a host, throwing a party on behalf of myself. Thus, I choose my team personally. And carefully."

"I see. Rough timing with Ms. Sanchez being out of commission so close to the end of your term." Adeline had never met Jada Sanchez in person, but anyone who'd even so much as looked at buying a streamer in Manhattan knew the woman's name. She was remarkable, not only for her A-list clientele but also for her staunch commitment to never expanding her company. She was a one-woman show, which was impressive, to be sure, but had left her clients without a party planner during her maternity leave.

"You know, it's strange," he said in a musing voice. "It's almost as though her unborn twins didn't take my status as mayor into consideration when choosing their birth date."

She was pleasantly surprised by his willingness to mock his own celebrity status. Her father had had exactly zero sense of humor when it came to the prestige of his position. In fact, her father probably would have quite literally resented Jada's children for daring to come into the world at a time that inconvenienced him.

"Nervy of those babies," Adeline said with a smile, playing along. "Perhaps they simply missed the memo that you're also Man of the Year?"

His flinch was so brief she nearly missed it, but it told her plenty about how he felt about *that* particular honor. Yet another surprise.

"I have to ask, do you even need an event planner with so little time left in your term?"

He didn't flinch this time, but the light in his eyes seemed to dim in a way that made her think he loved being mayor as much as he disliked being Man of the Year. "It's actually *because* of the end of the term that I need an event planner," he responded. "I'd like to have one last hurrah, or whatever you want to call it. I've enjoyed hosting here. Having people in my home gives me a chance to connect with them as a person, rather than simply a mayor."

"I'm sure you think so. But trust me, they're always *quite* aware that you're the mayor," she said, before she could stop herself.

He let out a surprised laugh. "If I may say, you seem a little hard to impress, Ms. Blake. I'm going to go out on a limb here—did you not vote for me?"

His voice was teasing, so she smiled in response. "I'm afraid I was denied the opportunity. I actually wasn't a New York City resident during either of your elections."

"Where are you from?"

Her smile never wavered, even as she avoided the question and pulled out her tablet to take notes. "I don't want to take up too much of your time, so perhaps get right to why I'm here. The party?"

He smiled blandly in response. "Of course."

Adeline nodded, careful to hide her relief at having dodged the need to give any details about her personal history. "What sort of timeline are you thinking for the event?"

He nodded. "Ideally within the next few weeks."

"Cocktail? Formal dinner?"

"Cocktails. No sit-down dinner, but enough food for people not to leave hungry if they don't want to. I'd been contemplating black tie. Go out in style, and all that."

She nodded and wrote it down, then looked up. "And why me?"

"Why you what?"

"Why am I sitting across from you right now instead of one of the city's many event planners?" She asked it casually, knowing the question could be viewed as simple curiosity on how he'd found her, but it was a hell of a lot bigger than that. She wanted to know if *he* knew he was hiring Addie Brennan.

The damn man gave nothing away. "How do you know you're not one of many being interviewed?"

"Am I?" she asked.

His eyes narrowed, and she knew she'd pushed far enough.

She put on her best professional smile and backpedaled. "I apologize for asking so many questions. It's just not every day a relatively new event planning company gets a call from the mayor's office. It caught me by surprise."

"A pleasant surprise?" he asked in a teasing voice.

She gave him a deliberately impassive smile and said nothing.

The mayor shrugged. "My campaign manager recommended you. He attended a retirement party for one of his wife's colleagues recently that you hosted."

"Oh? Do you remember the name?" She watched him carefully for any indication that this was all a sham to get close to the governor's daughter.

"No."

Strangely, it was the blunt answer that had her shoulders relaxing slightly. A politician with an angle would have gathered every detail and delivered a scripted answer down to the color of the tablecloths at said party. Instead he seemed merely a busy man who needed an event planner in a hurry and had taken the first business card passed his way. And she had hosted a retirement party just two weekends ago, fabulous enough to warrant attention, if she did say so herself.

"You know, Ms. Blake, I confess I was under the impression that this meeting was an interview, and it is. But I had it backward, didn't I? *You're* interviewing *me*. Not the other way around."

She smiled and answered honestly. "I can't pretend working for you wouldn't make for lovely bragging rights."

"But?"

"But," she continued, "I factor in other criteria when determining workload for me and my team."

He blinked. "Team? So it wouldn't be you specifically working on the party?"

"I sometimes delegate. Does that bother you?" She studied him, again looking for any tip-off that his reasons for wanting to hire her were politically motivated.

He merely shrugged. "I respect the need to delegate tasks. What's your other criteria?"

"Headache potential," she replied. "I like to evaluate potential clients based on how many Excedrin I think I'll need at the end of the event."

"How am I doing on that scale so far?" He smiled boyishly in a way that she suspected he knew was ridiculously appealing. Because it *was* ridiculously appealing. Even to someone as jaded on politicians as herself.

Careful, Adeline. You know better than anyone that politicians are never what they want you to think.

"To be determined," she answered.

"And if I promise to behave? To be a zero-Excedrin client?" he prompted, smile widening. "Do I have a new event planner?"

He was damn sure he did—she could tell by the cocky tilt of his grin.

The smile was compelling as hell, and he knew it. Just like she knew she'd never take this job until she could establish they were on equal ground. And for that, the mayor needed to be knocked down a peg or two. To let him know that her company had enough going on that they didn't drop everything because the Man of the Year crooked his finger.

Adeline's smile was all polished professionalism as she stood. "I'll have to assess my team's availability. I'll be in touch."

He let out a startled laugh as she turned and headed toward the door, but he called her name before she could escape to the safety of the hallway. "Ms. Blake."

She glanced over her shoulder and locked gazes with him, watching as the green in his eyes disappeared completely so that they seemed to glow pure gold as he looked at her.

"See that it's *your* availability you're checking," he said softly. "Not your team's."

It was more command than request, and it should have set off alarm bells. And it did. But not because it signaled a high-handed element to his personality. And not even because it could be a sign that he knew who she really was.

But because it did something strange to her lower stomach. Something that had nothing to do with him as the mayor and her as an event planner.

Chapter Three

"Mr. Mayor?"

Robert swiveled his conference room chair slightly toward the education lobbyist and pretended that his preoccupation had to do with the subject at hand instead of the woman who'd left his office two hours earlier. He set his palm on top of the proposal in front of him and gave an assertive nod. "I like what I've heard. I look forward to reviewing it more carefully later this week."

It wasn't a lie. Not a total lie, anyway. He *had* liked what he'd heard about expanding New York schools' music programs. Until he'd tuned out.

Robert was more than a little chagrined to realize his attention had wandered elsewhere mid-presentation, and since the issue was too important to pass judgment on without knowing the details, he had to put it off until he could read up on the parts he'd missed.

God, he wished Kenny were back. His chief of staff was the master of knowing when Robert's brain was juggling too many issues at once and knew how to steer him to the topic at hand. Of course, the issues usually fighting for attention in Robert's brain were work related.

He couldn't claim that now.

Carol Grinks opened her mouth, looking ready to argue, but then her mouth clicked shut. She was assertive and smart. And she'd apparently worked with Robert long enough to know when to push and when to bide her time. She stood, and her team followed suit. "Thank you for your time," Carol said. "I'll be in touch."

Robert nodded in acknowledgment as they exited the conference room together, grateful for the reprieve. Grateful that one of the city's most prominent lobbyists hadn't realized his source of distraction wasn't an opposing issue but a certain brunette who, in the span of their twenty-minute meeting, had managed to intrigue him in a way no woman had for months.

Months? Who was he kidding? It had been *years*. Hell, for that matter, had he *ever* responded so immediately to a woman as he had the moment Adeline Blake had stepped into his office?

Strictly speaking, she'd looked almost identical to the woman in the photo Martin had shown him yesterday. Her dark hair had been tied into a knot at the back of her head, and her clothes had been that of a career woman who played it safe with her wardrobe, her makeup subtle enough that his male eye didn't have the faintest clue if she wasn't wearing any or had just mastered the look of *looking* like she wasn't wearing any.

She hadn't been flashy. She hadn't been provocative. She hadn't been the Addie Brennan of the tabloids.

But whatever she *had* been was alluring as hell.

It had been a strange type of torture having to sit across the desk from her, discussing timelines and dress code for a party, when all he'd wanted to do was lean forward and tug that tidy bun from its confines and see how long her hair was. Would it fall all the way down her back? Just to her shoulders? Would it be as soft as it looked? As soft as the curves he suspected she was hiding under the blazer?

Robert gave a grunt of irritation at his thoughts and ran a hand through his hair. What was wrong with him? Not only had he completely failed to glean any information on why she'd changed her name to Adeline Blake, but he also hadn't even remembered she *was* the governor's daughter.

Martin would be annoyed, but not nearly as annoyed as Robert was with himself. One of the reasons he was so good at his job was because he'd been immune to exactly this sort of distraction for eight years. He'd been in the game long enough to know that more than a few of the clichés about the political arena held uncomfortably true. Power was abused, mistresses were almost expected, and plenty of officials were far more concerned with where their next vote came from than they were with the issue at hand.

Robert had always prided himself on rising above. He was here to serve the people, not rule them. He'd dodged every seduction attempt that had come his way, and as he'd told Martin, he'd made it a point to not worry about the next job until the current one was complete.

But apparently, all it took was one gorgeous brunette who'd shown zero interest in working with him, much less flirting with him, to command all of his thoughts.

He shook his head and headed back to his office, intending to have a firm pep talk with himself about how he was the damned mayor of New York City, not a high school kid with a boner for the new girl in class.

His assistant was standing in the entrance to his doorway, a takeout bag in hand.

"What's this?" he asked, when she handed him the bag.

"You didn't eat lunch," Darlene replied.

Robert frowned. "I didn't?" Apparently he was even more distracted than he'd realized.

"You didn't. I got you a BLT with extra avocado, and if Rita Gagnon calls with one of her lectures on plant-based diets, I promise to say you held the bacon. Do you know, last time she was in here, she pointed at my tuna sandwich and asked if I'd murdered any fish lately?"

"Yeah, well. If she had it her way, the entire city would be vegetarian."

"If she had it her way, the entire *country* would be *vegan*," Darlene said. "Anyway, Martin called. Four times."

"Sorry about that," Robert said tiredly. "I've asked him repeatedly to call my cell instead of bugging you."

"He said he tried that, and you weren't picking up. I pointed out that you were the mayor and had maybe one or two things on your plate aside from taking his phone calls. But you know how he is. Said it was urgent, but when is it not with him?"

Robert lifted his eyebrows. He was used to Darlene speaking her mind. He encouraged it. But she was usually a bit more subtle. "I take it we're not a fan of Martin these days?"

"These days?" she muttered.

"I'll talk to him," Robert said. "I know he can be overbearing when he wants something, but he needs to know when to pick his battles, and with whom to pick them."

"Thank you, sir," she said with a relieved smile.

Sir. Eight years, and he *still* wasn't used to that. He knew it was protocol, but a little part of him wondered what it would be like to simply be Robert.

He thanked Darlene for the late lunch and told her to head out for the day. Shutting the door to his office, he set the bag on the desk but didn't take out the sandwich. It was nearly five now; he may as well wait another few minutes and call the sandwich a working dinner as he went through his emails.

The prospect was slightly more depressing than it had been a year ago, when takeout inhaled in front of the computer had been the norm—something to sustain him between meetings, networking, and strategizing. He'd never minded in the past. Robert loved his job. He still did. It was just that with the end right around the corner, he was increasingly aware of just how little he had going on *outside* of work.

He had plenty of friends, but lately he'd wondered how many of them would still invite him to golf if he could no longer grant political favors. How many would feed his dog when he went out of town?

Not that he had a dog. No time for that. Certainly no time for a girlfriend. Getting laid, on the other hand . . .

That was becoming all too pressing a need. This afternoon had made that painfully clear.

He'd half-heartedly pulled up his in-box and just started to unwrap his sandwich when Martin came charging through his office door.

With a silent grunt of protest, Robert tossed the sandwich aside, appetite gone.

"You've been dodging me." Martin dropped unceremoniously into the chair opposite his.

"I've been busy." *Sort of.*

"Right," Martin said, as usual getting right to the heart of whatever he deemed most important, regardless of what anyone else had going on. "So, what's the scoop?"

"Scoop?" Answering a question with a question was a stalling tactic usually reserved for press conferences, and Martin knew it, because his brown eyes narrowed on Robert for a moment before clarifying. "The Brennan girl," Martin said. "How'd the meeting go?"

Well, let's see, I can't stop thinking about bending her over my desk, so there's that . . .

Robert shrugged. "Not much to report."

"Bullshit," Martin said. "She's Addie Brennan, for God's sake. That girl was never able to walk into a room without turning something upside down."

"Well, she's not a girl any longer," Robert said, carefully keeping the irritation at Martin's condescension out of his voice.

Martin's smile turned lascivious. "No?"

Robert wanted to knock the lewd grin right off Martin's face. He closed his eyes to rein in his irritation. *Get. A. Grip.*

"You think she suspected you knew her real name?"

Robert was a little embarrassed to admit to himself he hadn't really given this as much thought as he should, so he considered it now. "I don't know," he answered finally. "She definitely seemed interested in learning how I'd heard about her, but that also could have just been curiosity or caution."

Martin snorted. "Caution? You're the fucking mayor. She should have been on her knees trying to land the deal."

Robert heard a faint popping sound, then looked down, surprised to realize he'd cracked his knuckles without so much as a chance to stifle the urge.

He took a deep breath and tried to calm his temper and refocus on the reason Adeline Blake was on his radar in the first place. "She seemed pretty confident I wouldn't be looking at her as anyone other than Adeline Blake."

"She has a right to be confident," Martin said. "She did a damn good job covering her tracks. She ruthlessly eliminated every trace of Addie Brennan."

"Obviously not *every* trace. How'd you find her?" A little late to be asking, but he was curious about the woman in a way he hadn't been yesterday, when she'd been merely a name and a face in a photograph. Adeline Blake had been an intriguing mix of candor and subtle wit. The fact that she was a damned attractive woman hadn't escaped his notice, either, though he wished it had.

Martin lifted his eyebrows. "You don't usually want to know how the sausage is made."

Robert wasn't entirely sure he wanted to know now, either. At his core he was a control freak, but he'd learned early in his political career that to have a chance of making it in this world, he had to know when to delegate so he could focus his efforts on where they were needed. "Were your means illegal?"

"No," Martin answered automatically. "Absolutely not. You made it clear when you hired me that you played it straight, just like your dad did. I may look for loopholes in laws, but I never cut the rope."

Robert felt a pang in his chest at the mention of his father. At the reminder that the man had never had a chance to prove just how much he'd loved this city and helping people.

Martin was absolutely right—his dad had embraced clean politics, and Robert was aspiring to follow in his father's straight-as-an-arrow footsteps. But Robert Sr. had died before he'd even had a chance to tarnish the halo the whole damn city had placed on his head.

That halo had been transferred to Robert, and he'd bent over backward ensuring it stayed straight and shiny. But he was aware it could slip at any moment. Or rust. Or get thrown off altogether in sheer weariness at having to be so damn infallible all the time.

Robert had been only fourteen when his father had died at age forty-one. New York royalty struck down in his prime by a brain aneurysm just weeks before the mayoral election. Robert was thirty-five now, and terrified he was playing a losing game against time.

How long could one man play at perfection?

"And what sort of loophole led you to the realization that Addie Brennan and Adeline Blake were one and the same?" Robert asked, dragging his attention back to his father's former junior campaign manager—a man Robert was seriously wondering if his father would have kept around if he'd known just how low Martin seemed willing to go at times to achieve his goals.

"Luck," Martin surprised him by admitting. "She was on the local news a few weeks back talking about planning the perfect Labor Day party, or some such."

"A bold move for someone trying to keep her real identity a secret."

Martin nodded in agreement. "She almost got away with it. I thought I knew everything there was to know about Addie Brennan, but I'd been watching the girl talk for a good ten minutes and didn't figure it out. Good thing I've got a behavioral psychiatrist for a wife."

"Sandra figured it out?" Robert asked in surprise.

"Not right away. But the entire time we were watching, she kept insisting the event planner reminded her of someone. Bad luck for Addie that Sandra was writing a research paper on whether or not mannerisms are hardwired into our DNA. Adeline may not *look* like Addie, she may not *act* like Addie, but apparently she tilts her head in the same way and makes the same gestures when she speaks. Sandra figured it out a couple days later in the middle of the night, delighted to have put the pieces together. Needless to say, I treated her to a very nice dinner that night. Come to think of it, I should expense it to your office. Her realization may have won you the governor's election."

"Don't get ahead of yourself," Robert said. "We haven't officially started the campaign yet, and having met Adeline Blake, I'm not sure she's going to be the open book you were hoping for."

Martin waved a hand. "So she's a good actress. It was only the first meeting. I didn't really expect her to make it easy for us."

"What *were* you expecting?"

"To be honest, I wanted to know if she'd even show up. She had to know she'd be walking right into the lion's den."

If she had known, she hadn't shown it. Adeline Blake had acted every bit the part of a professional career woman testing the waters with a new client, not a wild child looking to thwart her father by cavorting with his enemy.

"We've got time," Martin said. "Eventually, she'll let her guard down, slip up at some point. Everyone does."

"What exactly is it you're hoping will happen?"

Martin held up his hands. "I told you, I've got no intention of exploiting the woman. But it's no secret that Addie and her father parted ways with no love lost, and nobody knows where the hell she's been for the past few years. If anyone's got dirt on Brennan, it's her. And I'd bet both nuts she'd be the only one bold enough to spill the dirt."

"You had a vasectomy. Do you even need the nuts?" Robert asked innocently.

Martin gave him the finger.

"All right, let's say she does have dirt," Robert said, picking up his sandwich when his stomach rumbled. "And let's say there's enough bad blood between her and her father that she'd be willing to go on the record to say what she knows. Why the hell would she tell us?"

"Not us. You. It's long past time you put that pretty face to use with a woman."

Robert tossed his sandwich aside once more. "I'm not going to seduce a woman for information. This isn't wartime, and I'm not a damned secret agent."

"Fine. But you're too smart not to know we've got to keep an eye on this girl. For all we know, she and her father have mended things, and she showed up with an agenda to get close to you."

"Well, then, great plan on bringing her into my office so I could hire her to plan a party in my fucking house," Robert said.

"Keep your enemies closer, and all that. So you hired her?"

"Tried to."

"What do you mean, you tried to?"

Robert shrugged. "She said she had to check her schedule. To be honest, I'm not holding my breath. I know a blow off when I see one."

Martin looked nonplussed. "She said no to the opportunity to plan the send-off party for the most popular mayor in the history of the city?"

Robert shrugged, because truthfully, he was a little impressed that she hadn't jumped all over the opportunity to work with him. Too often he found himself wondering if the people who surrounded him even liked him, or if they were there for what he could do for them.

Exposure. Bragging rights. Or everybody's favorite euphemism for kissing ass: networking.

Adeline Blake had wanted nothing to do with him, and that fact had been surprisingly enticing.

His campaign manager exhaled. "Robbie. We ran another focus group this afternoon. Everyone still adores you, but everyone also adores the governor and are hot for the fact that he has more experience. I know you don't like it, but son . . . we need to know what that girl knows."

Chapter Four

Ultimately, Robert wasn't exactly sure what drove his decision to seek out Adeline Blake: a desire to see if Martin was right about her having inside knowledge of her father's misdeeds, or a different sort of desire entirely.

He didn't even know which was worse, given her real identity: political motivation or personal interest.

He *did* know that once he made the decision and got into the car, regret was nowhere to be found. Only anticipation.

As mayor, he made it a point to spend as much time as possible out of the mansion. In order to run the city, he had to *know* the city. As often as his schedule permitted, he took lunches in Brooklyn, made on-site appointments in Queens and the Bronx, even tried to make it out to Staten Island to talk with the law enforcement officials in their backyard, not his.

But as much as Robert considered himself an expert on New York City, he had to admit that the trendy SoHo neighborhood was a bit of a blind spot for him. As a centerpiece of the New York fashion world, it was best known for its high-end shopping. And since Robert wore mostly suits, and had most of those custom made by a local guy in the

Bronx, he rarely had cause to visit the stylish neighborhood named for its location south of Houston Street.

Today, he definitely had a reason. And her name was Adeline Blake.

The town car pulled to a stop, and Robert glanced in surprise out the window. "This is it?" he asked his driver.

"Yes, sir. The address you gave me is just up on the right."

Robert glanced in the direction Tim pointed and saw only an expensive-looking storefront with purses in the window. It didn't look like a quintessential office space, but then, few things in New York City looked like what they should. And he trusted Darlene enough to know she wouldn't have given him the wrong address.

Climbing out of the car, he nodded at the bodyguard who was already patiently waiting on the sidewalk. Robert had a rotating set of NYPD officers who served as his security detail. They were all exceptional officers, but there was one man whom Robert trusted with his life above all others. He'd first hired Charlie Wilkiers on his own dime in the months leading up to the first mayoral election, when threatening letters had made it increasingly clear that a higher profile meant a higher risk. He'd hired Charlie first and foremost as a bodyguard, but the man had also become a trusted friend over the years.

"Looks like it's on the second floor above the shop, sir. Gayle's already upstairs, finishing her sweep," Charlie said, opening the door.

"Thanks," Robert said. He seriously doubted there was much in the way of threats in an event planner's office in SoHo. Especially one who didn't know he was coming. But he respected the necessity of the routine.

The elevator looked small and slow, so Robert opted for the staircase up to the second floor. There were two doors, one for a therapist, the other labeled JET SET EVENTS.

He nodded at Gayle, a petite redhead who looked like she couldn't lift a doughnut, but who Robert had once seen take down a purse snatcher twice her size.

He opened the door to Adeline's office and blinked in surprise. He didn't know what he'd been expecting when he'd pictured entering her domain, but it definitely wasn't this. The space was spacious and minimal, and yet unmistakably feminine. It wasn't fussy in a way that would make male clientele uncomfortable, but the deep red and black color scheme, the throw pillows that looked like some sort of faux fur, and even the lush-looking area rug gave the entire room a sumptuous feel.

"Hello! How can I—" The receptionist behind the front desk broke off as she glanced up and saw him more fully. She bolted to her feet, her rolling chair shooting backward. "Oh my goodness. You're the—Oh my gosh!"

"Don't salute," he instructed with a friendly smile, when he saw her right hand fluttering around her side.

She put the same hand to her chest with a nervous laugh. "I was so about to do that. How did you know?"

"It happens more often than you'd think," he said to reassure her, and because it was true. Most people didn't know what the heck to do when they came face-to-face with an elected official, especially one with as much authority as the mayor.

"Mr. Mayor?" she said, taking a tentative stab at the right address.

"That's me. And you are . . ."

"Cordelia." She pulled her chair back in, less flustered now. "I'm so sorry, did you have an appointment? Both Becky and Luciana have off-site client meetings. Adeline's in, but meeting with someone at the moment."

Robert's gaze scanned the office space behind the reception desk, noting that there were three doors. Two off to the left with the nameplates BECKY MERIDAN and LUCIANA RODRIQUEZ on the doors, the other with Adeline's name. All three had EVENT PLANNER printed in small letters beneath their names.

He smiled wryly, wondering if she'd talked to her employees about taking him on as a client, or simply decided he was too-many-Excedrin worth for any of them to deal with.

"Do you know how long Ms. Blake will be?" he asked Cordelia, nodding toward Adeline's door. "I'm happy to wait."

Cordelia sat back at her computer and, a couple of clicks of the mouse later, glanced up. "The client that's in there now is scheduled until three, but I'm happy to check with her when she's done and give you a call if she's got a moment."

"I'll wait," he said, gesturing toward the plush seating area.

"Oh," she said, with enough panic in her tone to have him pausing. "Actually, Adeline—Ms. Blake—prefers that her client meetings not overlap. It ensures everybody's privacy."

He smiled in bemusement. "She's an event planner. Aren't parties by their very nature *un*-private?"

She gave a small smile that told him there was plenty he didn't know about this world, and her next words confirmed it. "You'd think," Cordelia said. "But for a lot of people, the entire reason for hiring an event planner of Jet Set's caliber is the exclusivity of it. Everyone wants their party to be *the* event of the year. Let's just say it keeps things simpler to keep people separate."

"Ah. Politics. I'm vaguely familiar." He winked, and she giggled. Robert found himself wishing Cordelia's boss found him half as charming.

Still, he must not have been that charming. Adeline's assistant seemed *very* determined to throw him out.

"What if I promise to sit there and close my eyes when the current client comes out?" he said.

Cordelia smiled politely but stubbornly. "There's a great coffee shop around the corner. Or I can recommend a handful of restaurants nearby, and I'd be happy to give you a call if and when she's available."

Huh. No special treatment, then. Robert was strangely impressed, even though the agency's rules were mucking with his agenda of seeing Adeline.

But he understood as well as anyone the importance of organizing the flow of people in the appropriate manner, so he nodded. "She has my number. Tell her to text me when she gets a spare moment."

He put subtle emphasis on *when*. There was no *if* about it. Robert fully intended to see Adeline Blake again. And soon. But he didn't want to hound her assistant about it, especially since he was already going to be on one woman's bad side for showing up without an appointment— he didn't want to annoy *two*.

Robert had turned toward the door, resigned to grabbing a coffee around the corner as he'd been instructed to do, when Adeline's office door opened to the soft sound of feminine laughter.

He turned back just in time to see Cordelia's eyes go wide in panic at the realization that she'd failed to adhere to her boss's rules of no overlapping clients. Robert felt for the receptionist, but short of diving for the door, there wasn't much he could do—both of the other women had already spotted him.

Adeline's laughter died on her lips immediately when their gazes collided.

The other woman's smile remained, although it turned catlike, almost calculating, as she studied him. She was beautiful, in a statuesque kind of way. Tall and thin, with sharp, pale patrician features adding to the impression that she should be carved out of marble and haughtily looking down at museum patrons in the Louvre.

"Mr. Mayor," the woman said, with none of the nervousness or awe he usually encountered from people he'd just met. "What an *interesting* surprise." She all but purred it, her curiosity palpable. "Are you a client of Adeline's, or are you here for more personal reasons?"

It was an inappropriate question, uttered by a woman he was betting didn't believe societal rules or niceties applied to her.

Adeline's lips pressed together slightly, and he knew he'd stuck her between a rock and a hard place. She hadn't taken him on as a client, and though he fully intended to change her mind, he wouldn't do so by trapping her. But neither did he want rumors of them dating floating around. For him, it'd be political suicide if her real identity was ever leaked. For her, well . . . judging from the scowl on her face, she'd just as soon die as be connected personally to him, even allegedly.

So, he used a go-to political trick and threw up a smoke screen.

Letting a slow smile develop, he stepped toward the woman. "I'm afraid you have me at the disadvantage. You know me, but I don't know that I've had the pleasure." He *may* have let a deliberate amount of charm slip into his voice.

Adeline apparently heard it, and saw it for what it was, because she rolled her eyes behind the other woman. However, his target either missed or welcomed his maneuvering, because her smile turned even more feline as she stepped toward him and extended a hand the way a queen would to a subject. "Melora Manchester. We haven't met personally, no, but I believe you knew my late husband?"

Robert hid his surprise, but just barely. Hank Manchester and his first wife—a kind, if opinionated elderly couple who loved New York City almost as much as they'd loved each other—had been one of his biggest campaign donors for his first term. Judith Manchester had passed away suddenly, shortly after Robert had been elected, and though he vaguely remembered hearing that Hank had remarried, he'd never met the second wife, though he'd heard rumors that she was much younger than Hank. Seeing the second Mrs. Manchester now, he saw that his sources had understated the age difference. This woman didn't look a day over forty, but Hank had passed away at eighty-six a few months back.

His smile never wavered as he shook her hand, trying not to be irritated that she held his grip much longer than necessary. "I'm sorry to hear about your husband. He was one of this city's treasures."

"*My* treasure," she said, setting her left fingers to trembling lips.

He didn't want to assume her grief was forced, but the lack of wedding ring didn't exactly sell the grieving-widow routine. Neither did the unmistakable invitation in her eyes a mere three months after her *treasure's* passing.

"It was a pleasure to finally meet you in person, Mrs. Manchester," Adeline said, apparently deciding she'd had enough of the show, and plainly dismissing the woman. "I or one of my colleagues will be in touch by the end of the week regarding the celebration of your fiftieth."

Robert bit back a laugh at the murderous look Melora shot Adeline over her shoulder. Adeline merely smiled politely, but he'd bet the age-drop hadn't been accidental.

"Please do," Melora said, her forehead smoothing out once more as she turned back to Robert. "I think I'll *very* much enjoy being on your roster."

Robert maintained his smile, though he was tempted to tell the other woman that if there was any room on Adeline Blake's roster, he'd be taking the spot.

Adeline gave Melora a noncommittal smile. "Cordelia will make sure we have your updated contact information. Now if you'll excuse us, as you can see, my three o'clock is here."

Adeline stepped aside, giving Robert room to slip past the scheming widow and enter her office. Her professional smile never left her face, though her eyes narrowed just slightly as they met his, and he knew he'd gotten past her gates only on a technicality. He was the lesser of two evils when compared to Melora.

"Your three o'clock appointment, huh?" he said under his breath, after he'd stepped into her office and she'd closed the door behind him.

"Don't get excited," she muttered. "It'll most definitely be your last."

Chapter Five

Adeline didn't bother to soften her glare as she rounded her desk. "A surprise drop-by, Mr. Mayor? I have to admit I thought you were above that."

"I hadn't heard from you. Thought you may have lost my phone number."

"It's been twenty-four hours," she said in exasperation. "I told you I'd check our availability and get in touch."

He merely grinned. "May I sit?"

She didn't bother to reply since he was already taking a seat.

The majority of Adeline's clients were women, so she didn't get a lot of men visiting her office. The mayor should have looked out of place in the feminine space, but instead he looked perfectly at home in a gray suit and blue tie, sitting in her leopard-print guest chair. The business side of Jet Set might be Adeline, but the office itself was pure Addie.

She'd known from the start that getting an event planning business off the ground in a crowded, competitive market like New York would mean long hours. And if she had to spend long hours in a place, she wanted to love it, and she wanted it to look like her brand. Lush, expensive, and extravagant.

Ultimately, it had taken most of her savings and left next to nothing for furnishing her tiny one-bedroom apartment, but a little more than a year into her business, she was already starting to see the payoff. Much as women like Melora Manchester drove her crazy, they had deep pockets, bustling social lives, and a distinct penchant for exactly the type of luxurious feminine branding Adeline's office conveyed. It was the same reason she'd spent an exorbitant amount of money on silk-coated business cards with rose-gold embossing. It wasn't just about passing along her contact information. It was about selling a style. A style that she wasn't at all sure how to fit to the extremely masculine presence sitting across from her.

"So, Mr. Mayor. What is it you hoped to accomplish by this uninvited office-crashing?" she asked.

"Harsh," he said with a grin that showed he wasn't the least bit offended. In fact, the man looked exceedingly pleased with himself. "But to answer your question, I'm looking for a simple yes or no, Ms. Blake. Actually, that's not true. I'm looking for a yes. But if you are going to peddle me a no, I need to know sooner than later so I can make alternate arrangements with a competitor."

She carefully hid her frustration, not at him, but at herself. Adeline wanted to say yes for the right reasons. Because planning a party for the mayor and current Man of the Year was a résumé booster a smart businesswoman simply wouldn't pass up. A black-tie event, with what she was assuming would be an unlimited budget, unless rumors of the mayor's wealth were exaggerated, was exactly the sort of game changer a still-new company like hers should leap at.

However, Adeline wasn't just in charge of doing what was best for Jet Set; she was also tasked with keeping her Addie side in check. Addie, who wanted to say yes for all the *wrong* reasons, starting with the most annoying one: the damn man gave her butterflies.

"Why didn't you tell me you had an office?"

"What?" she asked, distracted. "Of course I have an office."

"Do your clients meet you here?"

"For consultations and planning sessions, yes. For on-site meetings when I need to see the space for an event, obviously we meet at the venue."

"You came to my office yesterday."

"So *very* observant of you, Mayor Davenport." The sarcasm slipped out, and she realized she didn't care. Conversation with this man felt like a puzzle; she needed to distribute her mental energies appropriately.

"Why didn't you make me come here?"

She gave him a look. "Does anyone make you do anything? You're the mayor, which was made quite clear to me when Mr. Tillman summoned me to your court."

"It's a great space," he said, not denying or apologizing for Martin Tillman's expectation that *she* go to the *mayor*. "Your office, I mean."

"Thank you," she said, feeling a genuine rush of pleasure at the compliment. "I know conventional business wisdom says you should start small with a brand-new company, but I knew from the beginning that if I wanted to create a luxury brand, I had to *look* like a luxury brand."

He nodded in understanding. "That's what business loans are for. Allows people with a good head on their shoulders to build something they wouldn't normally be able to afford in the early stages."

"Actually, I financed myself. Well, sort of. My mom left me some money when she passed, and I thought the best way to honor her was by throwing it into something that she loved."

His face took on a strange expression, which she assumed was the usual knee-jerk reaction to learning someone's parent had passed away. "Your mother was an event planner?"

Adeline immediately regretted her overshare. She rarely talked about her mom with anyone, and she certainly shouldn't be discussing Jeanette Fleming with *him*.

She fought the instinct to change the subject abruptly, since it would only draw more attention to the topic. She kept her tone as light as possible, hoping to convey mild indifference to the backstory of her career. "Not exactly. Well, not at all, actually. She was a waitress at one of the only restaurants in a small town. It was the default location for celebrations, from birthdays to wakes to end-of-the-year soccer parties. She always took it upon herself to make sure they were special. Stuff that went way above her job description. Balloons, flowers, even taught herself how to make fancy cakes. I guess that always just . . . appealed to me."

He continued to study her with an intent expression. "She taught you the tricks of the trade, huh?"

Sure. Once I realized she hadn't died in childbirth, like my bastard of a father claimed.

Adeline shrugged. "I didn't realize at the time I was being taught. I started out just helping at the hostess desk or busing tables on busy nights at the restaurant. But then she got sick a couple years ago, and I was helping more and more. Then she passed away, and long story short, I couldn't bear to be in the town where I seemed to see her everywhere. So, I moved to New York last year, and I took up her trade, but in my own way." She kept her eyes on the desk in front of her, blinking rapidly to keep the tears at bay. It had been a year and a half now, and the stabs of grief, while less frequent, still caught her by surprise.

Robert didn't say anything for a long moment, and she appreciated his giving her time to get her emotions back in check. People were always quick to want to comfort, and while she knew it was well-meaning, it sometimes only made things worse.

Finally, she lifted her eyes to his, and he nodded. A simple gesture that said plenty. *I'm sorry for your loss. You're going to be okay.*

It was exactly what she needed, especially from someone who understood loss firsthand. Robert Davenport Sr.'s sudden death while doing an interview on live television had shocked not just New York, but the entire country. She'd been just a girl when it had happened. Too young for her father to take her to the funeral, she, along with everyone else, had seen the pictures of stoic fourteen-year-old Robert Davenport Jr. laying a baseball mitt on his father's coffin. The photo had gone alongside tiny John F. Kennedy Jr.'s salute to his father's coffin as a heartbreaking moment in American history.

"So." She cleared her throat. "You knew Mrs. Manchester's late husband?"

"I did. He was a good man."

With horrible taste in women. It was an uncharitable thought, but she couldn't help it. Melora was grating and selfish and had very little respect for anyone else's time.

Come to think of it, she'd be a perfect match for Mr. Drop By with No Appointment.

"She's a client of yours?" he asked.

"I normally wouldn't confirm or deny, but since Mrs. Manchester already mentioned as much herself, she's hoping we'll take her on as a client, yes."

"I see. And how many Excedrin worth is she?" he asked.

She laughed, irrationally pleased at his recall of their conversation from the day before, wondering if he'd replayed it in his mind as many times as she had.

He leaned forward and lowered his voice to a conspiratorial whisper. "I bet lots. Way more than me."

"Oh, trust me, that's *very* debatable."

He leaned back again and placed one palm over the fist of his other hand, then let his hands drop to his lap and gave her a level look. "Just tell me what I did to get on your no list."

Too good-looking. Too confident. Too damn appealing. Oh yeah, and you belong in my father's world, which I want no part of.

"A black tie in three weeks? It's a big ask," she said. "And I already have people on my wait list."

He looked her directly in the eyes. "Bullshit."

"Excuse me?"

"No, I won't. I won't excuse you for chickening out on this. I believe you have your reasons, and that's fine, but don't sit there and tell me it's because you can't pull it off. That insults me and you."

That he was right was annoying. That he could read her so easily was alarming. That she wanted to say yes, not for the job opportunity, but because she felt strangely breathless when she was with him just plain ticked her off.

Caution, Addie.

"Why are you pushing this so hard?" she said, narrowing her eyes. "There are plenty of event planners in the city."

He gave her a steady look. "Because you made it abundantly clear yesterday you wouldn't kiss my ass. Call me crazy, but . . . I like that about you. I trust you to call me on my crap."

He stood to leave, and Adeline's stomach clenched in regret, but she forced herself to stand her ground and stay silent. To take the safe road.

"Call me if you change your mind," he said crisply.

"Robert," she blurted out.

Damn it. Just ten more seconds, and he'd have been out the door. "I'll do it."

He paused, then glanced over his shoulder, and it wasn't lost on her that he was mimicking her departure from his office yesterday.

Deliberate? Probably.

He grinned.

No. *Definitely* deliberate.

"I made reservations for lunch at two p.m. on Friday on the Upper East Side. We can discuss then. Darlene will email the details."

Her mouth dropped open. "What do you mean *reservations*? You didn't know I was going to say yes."

His grin went a little bit crooked and sexy as he looked at her. "See you on Friday."

Chapter Six

Adeline plucked two dresses out of her closet and turned toward her best friend. "Black or pink?"

"Black," Jane Kim said immediately. "It's your funeral."

Adeline rolled her eyes, but she did put the pink dress back in the closet. It was one of her favorites, but even with the conservative cut, it felt a little too feminine for the occasion.

The occasion being lunch with the mayor.

"If I draw you pictures of all the reasons this is a bad idea, *then* will you believe me?" her friend begged. "You always were a visual learner."

"Won't help," Adeline said, pulling her favorite pair of black pumps off the shoe rack. "You're a terrible artist."

"Not true. I won that drawing contest in third grade."

"Because everyone thought it was a thoughtful interpretation of a tornado. Had you told them you were actually attempting to draw a tulip, I think they'd have been less impressed."

"Talent is talent."

"And you have plenty of it," Adeline agreed loyally. "Just not in the fine arts category."

Adeline's best friend since the first grade, Jane had her master's in biomedical engineering and was the technology development officer at a stem cell research company headquartered in Tribeca. Brilliant, she was. Artistic, she was not.

But Jane was as loyal as they came. She, along with their friend Rosalie, was one of the precious few facets of Addie Brennan's life that had carried over to Adeline Blake's life.

Despite having grown up together upstate, Rosalie and Jane both found themselves living in the city, which had been a major reason why Adeline had decided to start her business in Manhattan, despite its relative proximity to her father.

Still, her friends knowing so much about her past came with some downsides. Jane, who'd been her friend the longest, was particularly protective of Adeline when it came to anything remotely associated with the governor. She had been there when Addie was growing up and had seen firsthand that the man the world saw was not the real version.

"I thought you swore you'd never get close to that world again," Jane called, as Adeline went into the bathroom to change. "You call politics the devil's work. Direct quote."

"I'm not getting into politics. I'm planning a party for someone who happens to be a politician. One and done."

"Uh-huh. You're telling me if Mr. Panty Melter turned those supernatural green eyes on you and asked you to plan another event, and then another, until he literally ate your soul for breakfast, you'd be able to resist?"

"There are so many *yikes* in that sentence, I don't know which to respond to."

Jane didn't back down. "What if your dad finds out that you're in New York? I mean, their paths must cross, right? Governor and mayor?"

Adeline froze for a second in the process of slipping her dress over her head, feeling slightly nauseous the way she did whenever she thought of her father. Then she took a deep breath and pulled the dress down. "He won't," she said, stepping into the bedroom and turning her back to her friend. "Zip me up?"

"So he still doesn't know you're here? Or about the name change?" Jane asked, pulling the zipper up.

"I have no idea," Adeline said. "I haven't had any contact with the man in five years. But I'm assuming not. If he did know, he'd probably have his thugs put a bag over my head in the middle of the night and leave me in a field somewhere."

"Bastard," Jane said with feeling. "I still can't believe he let you think for twenty-some years that your mother was *dead*—"

"Can we not?" Adeline interrupted gently.

"Right, right," Jane said quickly. "He's not worth the breath. But considering we don't even speak of your father, are you sure doing business with his biggest rival is smart? Wait. You're not doing this *because* the mayor's your father's biggest rival, are you?" Jane asked, brown eyes narrowing as she planted her fists on her hips.

"Of course not," Adeline said. "The mayor has no idea who I am, and he hasn't even confirmed he's entering the governor's race yet. I accepted the job because he's *Robert Davenport*. I'd be crazy to say no to *Citizen's* Man of the Year. His guest list alone will be worth the headache for the networking potential."

"Okay, fine. I can see why you can't resist taking him on as a client. But why does he want *you* as his party planner?"

Adeline gave her sometimes-too-blunt friend a look. "You want to rephrase?"

"You know what I mean," Jane said. "You're good, but you're also new. And to your point, he's *the* Robert Davenport. Why wouldn't he go with one of the big agencies for his fancy party? How can you be sure of his motives?"

"And I thought I was cynical," Adeline muttered. "Look, I asked him why he chose me, and apparently he likes the fact that I don't get all swoony in his company. Or something."

"And you believe him?"

"I can't afford not to believe him," Adeline said gently. "I get your concern. It's a big coincidence, and it's a risk. But my father's already taken enough away from me. I'm not going to let him take the biggest potential client away as well. If I get burned, I get burned. But at least I won't be off hiding in a tiny little corner of the country."

Not anymore, anyway.

Jane sighed as she followed Adeline into the kitchen. "Fine. I'll get on board. But only if you promise to share details. It's totally unfair that the guy is hot, successful in his own right, *and* born rich. Did you know he inherited like a billion dollars when his dad died? Not that that wasn't the saddest thing in the world. I'm just saying the guy's like Thor or something. Except instead of a magic hammer, he's got . . . well, I don't know. I wouldn't be surprised if he had a magic hammer, too, to go with all that money and pedigree. Now that I think about it, he's a little like Tony Stark."

Adeline gave her an amused look. "You're certainly up to date on the mayor's backstory."

"I read up on him in *Citizen* while I was at the dentist this morning."

"The same appointment that you're supposedly still at?"

Jane gave her a big grin. "I had to come try one last time to talk some sense into you in person. If my boss asks, I had a root canal."

"You've never had so much as a cavity. Or been grounded. Or gotten a pimple. Which, now that I think about it, why and how are we friends?"

"Opposites attract. Me: tiny, Asian rule follower. You: curvy, disorderly train wreck. How could we possibly resist each other?"

"A match made in heaven, for sure. But I'm reformed now, and we're no longer opposite. You going to dump me?"

"Never," her friend said. "Besides, we both know Addie isn't dead. She's just waiting for her phoenix moment."

Adeline's back was to Jane as she pulled her trench coat out of the closet, and she was glad her friend couldn't see her slight flinch. She didn't know which she was more afraid of—that her friend was wrong about her old ways waiting to make a resurgence, or that she was exactly right.

Because if that phoenix did rise, there'd be hell to pay.

Adeline had never been to the restaurant the mayor had picked for lunch, but she recognized the name. She'd half expected him to pick somewhere off the grid, or suggest their second meeting take place in his office, but apparently he had no qualms about meeting with her in public, because the restaurant was bustling, even at the late lunch hour.

Professional pride that she'd be seen having lunch with the most powerful man in the city warred with personal preservation—the need to protect. *Hide.*

Adeline lifted her chin. She'd already given up her name. She wouldn't add her career or her pride to the list of sacrifices.

She gave the hostess Darlene's name and was led to a table in the back of the room. Old habits had Addie immediately scanning for the mayor's protection, spotting the plainclothes officers who served as bodyguards immediately. Not the same faces she'd seen in his office on Tuesday. She wondered if that was intentional, to keep would-be attackers on their toes, or simply a function of the NYPD's internal structure.

The mayor rose when he saw her approach, a benign, if seemingly genuine smile on his face as he pulled out her chair.

"Pretty manners, Mr. Mayor."

He sat back in his own chair. "My mother will be pleased you think so. I believe she taught me that particular move when I was four."

"How is Mrs. Davenport?" Adeline couldn't stop herself from asking. The older woman had been an active part of her husband's career and had continued their charity work even after his death, but Adeline was pretty well plugged into that circuit these days, and she couldn't remember the last time she'd heard Katherine Davenport's name.

"She's great, thanks. Happy, healthy, shacking up with a not-so-secret boy toy in Florida." He waggled his eyebrows.

"My kind of lady," Adeline said as she placed her napkin in her lap, then instantly regretted it. A woman with a boy toy was *Addie's* kind of lady. Not Adeline's.

"Oh yeah?" he asked with a smile. "You've got a fleet of young bucks in the stable?"

"I'm pretty sure you're mixing your metaphors," she said.

"I'm pretty sure you're dodging the question."

She gave a coy smile over the top of her menu.

"Fine, Ms. Blake. Keep your secrets. For now."

For always, Mr. Mayor.

"Do you come here often?" she asked, recognizing the signs of a staff trained in providing as much privacy as possible for high-profile clientele.

"I like their gelato," he said, before gesturing for her to order a drink.

She narrowed her eyes. "Is that a line?"

He laughed. "A line? Exactly how cynical are you?"

"I figure you have a whole arsenal of casual statements like that in your back pocket to put people at ease so they think you're just a regular person."

The way he was looking at her made her want to shift in her chair, wondering if she'd given away too much.

"I am a regular person."

She snorted.

"All right, fine. I'm exceptional," he amended.

"Points for honesty. So, what kind of ice cream is your favorite?"

"*Gelato.* Crucial difference, Ms. Blake. It's made in-house daily, so whatever the flavor of the day is."

"And if you could choose?" A line appeared between his eyebrows at the question, and she laughed. "Nobody asks that, do they?"

"No. Most people seem rather charmed with my 'whatever they're serving' response."

Adeline shrugged. "I'm not most people."

"No. You're not." His gaze caught on hers, just a touch too intense for the moment, but she couldn't seem to make herself look away. Thankfully, someone arrived to refill their water glasses, and he broke the contact, clearing his throat. "Chocolate," he said. "I like chocolate."

"How original."

"I'm sure you meant to say *classic*."

She gave an amused smile and used it as a segue, pulling out her notebook. "Classic. Safe to say that's your party vibe?"

"I don't think I've ever been cool enough to have a *party vibe*." He said it jokingly, but there was a hint of regret there, and Adeline wondered if the pain of losing his father so young had come with a unique sort of pressure.

"You said three weeks until the party. I'm assuming you're looking at a Friday or Saturday, or is this a weekday thing?"

"I was thinking Saturday the twenty-fourth. Close enough to Election Day to be a proper finale to my tenure, without overshadowing the election itself."

She nodded and wrote it down. "Still thinking black tie?"

"I gave eight years of my life to these people. The least they can do is put on a bow tie or ball gown in thanks."

He smiled as he said it, and she studied him. "You do a lot of formal events?"

The mayor hesitated just for a moment. "I do. I guess you could say it's a legacy of sorts. I remember my parents always treated entertaining as though it were the highest honor and interacting with friends and voters was something to dress up for. I've always liked that. The idea of people dressing up for other people, best foot forward and all that."

"Anything your parents did at their parties that you'd do differently?"

His shoulders stiffened slightly, and she wondered if she'd overstepped. "I don't mean to be disrespectful," she said quietly. "But it's my job to create the perfect event for you. The more detail I have, the better."

The mayor took a sip from his water glass. "I like the dressing up and deliberateness of a formal event. I guess . . . I've sometimes wondered if there wasn't a way to build some relaxed fun in there, too. I don't understand why our best clothing has to bring out stiff behavior."

"Strapless bras," she said, without looking up from her notebook.

He set his water down. "Sorry?"

"The women are likely wearing strapless bras with their formal gowns. And/or Spanx. That's why they seem stiff."

She could have sworn his gaze drifted downward, and she was more than a little glad that her dress was a thick, conservative cut. *Nothing to see here.*

He shifted slightly in his chair, then jerked his chin at the menu in front of her. "Do you know what you'd like to eat yet?"

"Oh, no, I've barely looked. Have you?" she asked, glancing down at the menu.

"No, but I don't need to. I come here at least twice a week, and I always get the same thing."

"Seriously?"

He nodded. "The quinoa bowl, add salmon."

"Seriously?"

"You don't approve?"

"I'm all for healthy food choices, but I don't know that I could get excited about that twice or more in a single week."

The server seemed to sense their topic of conversation, because she approached from out of nowhere to take their order. Adeline opted for the butternut squash ravioli. As advertised, the mayor requested his usual.

"Do you drink wine?" he asked Adeline.

She hesitated. "I do, though not usually at client lunches."

"Might I suggest you're doing it wrong?" he said with a smile before turning back to the server. "If you still have that Chablis I had last week, we'll take a bottle."

Adeline blinked. "I can't share a bottle of wine with you."

"Why not?"

"It just looks . . . date-ish," she said, realizing how silly the protest sounded when she said it aloud.

He looked up at the waitress as she reappeared to open the wine and pour a small amount into a glass. "Do *you* think I'm on a date with this woman?"

"Mr. Mayor," Adeline said in a warning tone.

"No, sir, I do not," the brunette server said with just the slightest twitch of a smile.

"And why's that?"

The waitress smiled full-on now, obviously more comfortable with the mayor than Adeline had thought at first. "She just called you Mr. Mayor."

"My thoughts exactly. Not very romantic, is it?"

"No, Mr. Mayor."

Adeline rolled her eyes at him as the server filled both their glasses and left them alone once more. "Do you flirt with everyone?"

"In politics we call it *schmoozing*."

"Well, *schmooze* someone else. I'm here to do a job."

The mayor grinned, seemingly unperturbed. In fact, he looked rather pleased with himself, and more relaxed than she could ever remember her father or any of his colleagues looking. As though this was who Robert Davenport *was*, rather than who he pretended to be.

She picked up her glass and took a sip of the wine. It was excellent, of course. She put it aside. If she had any sense, she'd limit herself to one glass, certainly not half a bottle with this man who put her on edge when she was sober. She'd hate to see his effect on her if she were tipsy.

"Okay, let's talk details," she said, tapping her pen to her notebook. "Do you know if there are any contracts with caterers that I should be aware of?"

"For anything sponsored by the mayor's office, yes. Anything I host personally is paid for out of pocket by me. No rules or limitations."

"No limitations?" she asked.

He grinned. "Are you asking me your budget?"

"It's sort of a crucial detail."

"Let's just say you should feel free to book the best you can find."

"Huh. So the rumors are true," she said. Apparently she didn't need more than a sip of wine to feel bold.

"What rumors?"

She leaned forward. "You're successful, good-looking, *and* loaded."

He laughed. "What can I say, the media gets some things right."

Adeline shook her head and took another sip of her wine. "Honestly, how you've avoided getting dragged down the aisle is beyond me. You're like George Clooney before he met Amal."

"Maybe I just haven't met my Amal yet." His gaze flicked up to hers and locked.

Chapter Seven

Robert knew he'd caught Adeline off guard. Her eyes flared in surprise, her lips parting slightly.

He'd caught himself off guard, too. There was no earthly reason why he should be talking to an event planner about his romantic life. Or George Clooney's hot wife.

Nor should he be holding his event planner's gaze, trying like hell to figure out if she felt the same electric pull he did. He *definitely* should not be wanting to lean across the table and see if her mouth was as soft and sweet as it looked. Should not be wondering what sort of sounds she'd make if . . .

Adeline's surprise faded into a slow smile. One he didn't like. At all. He liked her next words even less.

"Oh my gosh," she said, her eyes widening, before she leaned forward. "I hope I'm not overstepping here, but I just realized you and my friend Rosalie would totally hit it off."

What the . . .

Robert took a sizable swallow of wine and set the glass back down on the table with a measured calm. "Are you attempting to set me up on a blind date?"

"You just mentioned you hadn't met the right woman yet," she said, still all wide-eyed innocence. "Rosalie's been on sort of this whole no-dating thing for years to focus on her career, but her company's just been bought out, so she's finally got some time to focus on her personal life. She's really great, truly."

Robert didn't care if the woman had Marie Curie's brain, Mother Teresa's heart, and Tina Fey's humor and was wrapped in Beyoncé packaging. The fact was he'd been sitting here fantasizing about what Adeline's body would feel like beneath his hands, and she'd been mentally evaluating his compatibility with her friend.

He'd never felt the sting of being friend zoned before, but he felt it now, and it was decidedly unpleasant. He was the mayor of the most populous city in the country, for God's sake. He was fucking Man of the Year. Generally, single women at least looked twice. They certainly didn't pass him off to their friend.

Most irritating of all was that some part of the back of his brain knew he should be relieved. Interest in Adeline Blake, elite event planner, was one thing. Interest in Addie Brennan, daughter of his future primary opponent and a ticking time bomb of potential scandal, was political suicide.

His hands lifted in the instinctive need to crack his knuckles, but he caught the gesture just in time, realizing how much the old habit seemed to be resurfacing these past few weeks. First with the Man of the Year nonsense, then with Martin's questionable strategy of cozying up to Adeline Blake in hopes of getting dirt on her father. Then with Robert's own out-of-character decision to go along with the plan.

But if eight years of being mayor had taught Robert anything, it was that every tactic came with a cost. Every win for the education budget meant a little less money for the mental health initiative. Every pop-up flu shot clinic meant there were fewer resources for the city's recycling program.

And every Election Day victory came with a cost.

Robert believed with his entire heart that there was something off about Governor Brennan. The man had rubbed him the wrong way since day one. He didn't like the way the governor spoke to staff members, the way he looked at women, and most especially, he didn't like the way the governor seemed to transform into an entirely different person when the cameras were on him. Having a "press face" was one thing, but Governor Brennan seemed to have a press personality. He became an entirely different person behind closed doors, and if the rumors were true, the cocky, grating man Robert had to deal with when the cameras were off was a veneer for an even uglier version.

Rumors that would stay exactly that, if they couldn't find someone on the inside willing to get out from under the governor's thumb.

Someone like the woman sitting across from him.

Exhaling, Robert mentally switched gears from man to politician. It wasn't particularly difficult. He'd quit putting his personal wants first the day after his father's funeral, when he'd committed to fulfilling his father's legacy. Everything else came second.

"I apologize," Adeline said, breaking the silence with a bland, distant smile that he hated, even though he understood it, as he had one of his own that he wielded when he was trying to control the conversation. "We're here to talk party details, and I'm playing matchmaker."

"It's fine," he said, responding with a deliberately cool smile of his own. "What else do you need from me in order to make this party happen?"

He had to give her credit—she was every bit as professional and focused on the art of event planning as Jada. For the next thirty minutes, he sipped wine and answered a seemingly never-ending string of questions.

How did he feel about caviar?
Thoughts on live music?
Dance floor or no?
Passed or tabled hors d'oeuvres?

Signature cocktails or stick to the classics?
Champagne label preferences?
Paper invitations or digital?
Did he have a calligrapher?
Guest list?
Parking?
Were there any outdoor spaces to work with?
Antagonistic relationships between guests to be aware of?
Coatrack?

In truth, it was all stuff that he could and probably should pass to Darlene, but he hadn't been lying when he'd told Adeline that he took pride in hosting the way his parents had. Granted, with his parents, it had been a joint effort. He remembered them sitting at the table with a bottle of white and notebooks, jokingly bickering about whether Judge Miller could really be trusted with cocktail sauce in a room with white carpet, or debating whether the rumors about an affair between so-and-so were viable enough to affect the guest list.

His father had known when to delegate in his professional life, but when it came to connecting with people, Robert Davenport Sr. had made hosting a personal priority. He'd wanted to know exactly who was coming into his home, what that person liked, what that person needed from him, and how to make sure that person left the party with a smile. And yes, a yea vote on Election Day.

Robert was fully aware that his success as a politician had come from mimicking this personal approach to public affairs. And currently, it gave him a legitimate excuse to stay close to Adeline Blake née Brennan.

She had her pen between her teeth as she studied her notes. "Okay, how about—"

"A break from the party talk?" he suggested. She looked up, and Robert nodded at her plate. "You've barely touched your pasta."

"Oh. Right." She put her notebook and pen aside with obvious reluctance and picked up her fork, taking a generous bite. "It's good," she said, pointing the fork down at the ravioli. "Really good. Better than your grass and beans, and don't try to tell me otherwise."

"Pretty hard to beat pasta," he said in agreement, pulling the bottle from the ice bucket and topping off both of their wineglasses.

She narrowed her eyes at him. "Are you trying to get me tipsy?"

"Do you have any meetings or events after this?"

She hesitated. "No."

"Me neither. So, what's the harm?" he asked, lifting his glass.

"Oh, I don't know. Me spilling my darkest secrets and saying things I shouldn't?" she said with a smile, punctuating the statement by picking up her water glass instead of the wine.

Bingo. Martin would practically be salivating at the lead-in, but Robert found himself hesitating, wishing that Adeline Blake would share her secrets with him someday because she wanted to—not because he pressed and plied her with alcohol.

He shook the sentimental longing aside. He was the mayor, soon to be the governor, if he played this right. He may be a clean politician, but he was still a politician. People like him weren't afforded the luxury of emotional indulgences.

The real question was, which was the right tactic with this woman? His attraction to Adeline made her hard as hell to read. On one hand, she was refreshingly forthright, so the direct approach could work well. On the other hand, she was also wary. If he pushed the wrong button, or pushed too hard, he could lose his chance to get his foot in the door altogether.

He did a mental coin flip and landed on the frank, get-right-to-it approach.

"Dark secrets, you say," Robert said, leaning forward with a deliberately casual grin. "Hard not to be intrigued. I've always had a weakness for a woman with a past."

The second the words were out, he knew his coin had landed the wrong fucking way. Her entire face seemed to shut down, her body going still like a trapped animal with no way out.

And not a scared, nervous doe. More like an angry, ticked-off lioness.

Adeline deliberately looked at her watch, then picked up her notebook. "Actually, Mr. Mayor, I'd love to stay and chat, but I think I have everything I need, and with the time crunch, I'd like to get started right away. If there's anything else you think of as it relates to your party, feel free to call my office. Cordelia will make sure any details get passed on to me. Thank you for the lunch. Now if you'll excuse me . . ."

He stood when she stood. "Ms. Blake—"

The chilling look she sent him froze his words in his throat. Just as well, since he obviously wasn't choosing the right ones when it came to this woman.

He cleared his throat. "Thank you for joining me."

She gave a cool, distant smile. "Thank you, Mr. Mayor."

He nodded in response as she walked away, even as everything felt wrong.

Chapter Eight

Robert walked into his office, his attention on his phone. He did a double take when he saw a man sitting in his chair.

The shock faded immediately into relief and happiness as the man spun fully around.

"Well, holy hell," Robert said with a grin, going to greet his chief of staff. "Look who was finally released from the shackles of early matrimony."

"If that's what you call a honeymoon, it's no wonder you're still single," Kenny Lamb said as the two men exchanged a quick thump of a hug.

"I thought you weren't back until next week. Wasn't the whole plan to have sex in the Caribbean for a week and then come back and have day sex in your apartment for the rest of the month?"

"It's called a staycation, and it's what all the cool kids are doing as a way of settling into married life in their own space, in a relaxing and productive manner."

"And you were bored?" Robert guessed.

"*Beyond* bored," Kenny said with feeling. "So was Melinda. She also thought her assistant choreographer was after her job and insisted she go down to the theater 'just to check on things.' That was four hours ago."

"Is she right? About her assistant angling for her job?"

"Probably. I've always said the only thing more cutthroat than New York politics is Broadway. Well, and the music scene. And Wall Street. Come to think of it, is your job even hard?"

"Not anymore," Robert replied. "My chief of staff is back."

"*Partially* back," Kenny clarified, dropping into a chair, the one opposite Robert's this time. "I won't officially be back until Monday, but in the meantime, entertain me. Darlene says Martin has been like a dog with a bone?"

"She'd be correct."

"What's the bone?" Kenny asked curiously.

Robert hesitated. He knew Kenny was better at his job when he had all the facts, however ugly they may be. He also knew that Kenny hadn't been able to stand Martin Tillman from day one. On more than one occasion, the usually affable Kenny had declared Martin "all that was wrong with the American political system."

The feeling was mutual. Martin was old guard and fancied himself the authority on all things Davenport. He took it as a personal affront that Kenny wasn't a "lifer," and that he hadn't personally known Robert Davenport Sr. To Martin, Kenny was an idealistic upstart with no respect for the elite legacy of the government.

Robert knew he needed both perspectives to bring in both sides of voters. He also knew that the Addie Brennan situation would only stoke a long-burning fire. He'd always made it a point to balance the perspectives of both men, but more often than not, when the two men disagreed, Robert's instincts told him to go with Kenny's perspective.

Kenny Lamb was, in most ways, an atypical chief of staff. Prior to coming on board to work with the mayor, Kenny'd had no government experience beyond his former career as a high school social studies teacher. He'd known how the government worked in theory, if not in practice, which had been exactly why Robert needed him.

There'd been plenty of smart, ambitious applicants angling for the chief of staff position, all clamoring to make a name for themselves. Kenny, looking for a career change to challenge himself, had merely wanted a chance to continue making a difference.

The happy-go-lucky thirtysomething hadn't been the obvious choice, but he'd been the right one. As it had turned out, Kenny hadn't just become indispensable to Robert on a professional level; the man had also become his closest friend. Kenny and his wife, Melinda, were a welcome respite from the whirlwind of public life, the people he'd always been able to count on to tell him when he'd gone off course, when he was losing sight of himself.

He knew it was Kenny who would tell him if his strategy with Adeline Blake was crossing a line that couldn't be uncrossed.

"I hired a new event planner," Robert said.

"I know," Kenny said, thumbing through his phone.

"You do?"

Kenny locked his phone and shoved it in his pocket, giving Robert his full attention.

"She wants to set me up with her friend," Robert blurted out, relieved that after stewing endlessly on the topic, he had someone to confide in.

Kenny was silent for a long moment. "You do realize I'm your chief of staff, correct? I've been away for weeks, and you're telling me that the most vital information right now is that you hired a new party planner, and that she's trying to set you up?"

Robert hesitated. It was the opening he needed to tell his friend the truth. He jerked his chin at the door. "Can you close that?"

Kenny did so, then sat again, looking calm and unruffled even though he knew Robert well enough to know when potential trouble was brewing. It was why Robert cherished his chief of staff so damn much. The guy was always the calm in the center of any storm.

"What's up?" Kenny nudged.

"The event planner—how'd you know I hired one?"

Kenny shrugged. "Darlene mentioned it offhand. Plus, I knew Jada was close to popping, and that you'd want to throw a party before you left office."

Robert shifted in his chair. "You know who she is?"

"Heard her name. Forgot her name." Kenny stretched out his legs, and slouched down in his chair, eyes closing as though settling in for a quick nap. "You just go ahead and wake me up when you're ready to spit out whatever's got you frowning."

"Her name is Adeline Blake," Robert said.

"Okay."

"Her real name is Addie Brennan."

Kenny's eyes popped open. "Brennan, as in . . . Governor Brennan?"

"His daughter."

Kenny took his time sitting up straight, but his gaze had turned sharp and aware. "*That* daughter?"

"That daughter."

"I thought she disappeared."

"She did. She's back."

Kenny chomped his gum. "Where's she been?"

"That's what I'm supposed to be figuring out."

"What do you mean that's what you're *supposed* to be figuring out?"

Robert hesitated, and Kenny picked up on it immediately.

"Martin's got a plan," Kenny said flatly.

"Always," Robert said with a slight smile.

The sharpness in his chief of staff's gaze didn't waver as he stared Robert down and waited for the explanation.

"Martin thinks the daughter's the best chance we've got on getting any dirt on the governor."

"*If* there's dirt."

Robert gave him a look. "C'mon. I know you're even more inclined than me to believe the best in people, but you can't think the rumors are just rumors."

Kenny shrugged. "They are until there's proof."

"Well . . ."

Kenny narrowed his eyes. "You've already got something?"

Robert hesitated. "I'm not sure."

"What is it?" Kenny asked, on high alert.

"You won't tell Martin?"

"I can't stand Martin. I wouldn't tell him if a bird pooped on his shoulder." Kenny's expression turned solemn. "And I won't say anything if it would hurt another person."

Robert ran his hands through his hair. "I know." And he *did* know. Kenny was as principled as they came, not just in terms of political maneuverings but as a person. Still, he hesitated, feeling strangely as though he was betraying Adeline by saying it aloud.

Remember, the only reason you even know Adeline is for this very reason.

"She mentioned her mother," Robert said, lifting his head.

Kenny blinked. "So? We all have one."

"I know, but . . ." Robert stared down at his thumbs, a quirky habit he'd gotten from his dad. His father had always very carefully lined up his thumbs alongside each other and studied them while gathering his thoughts. Finally, Robert looked up. "Addie Brennan didn't," he said quietly. "Or at least she wasn't raised by hers. The governor has always gone on record saying he was a widower, and that Addie's mother died in childbirth. If that story's true," he continued, "she wouldn't have any memories of her mother, and yet Adeline Blake most definitely does. *Fresh* memories of a woman who was a waitress and instilled in her a love of event planning. A woman who passed away recently."

Kenny blew out a breath and sat back in the chair. "Could be a woman she thought of as a surrogate mother?"

"Could be," Robert said. But his gut didn't think so. Adeline's grief had been unmistakable when she'd spoken of her mother, but her tone had also been matter-of-fact. He got the feeling that if this woman hadn't been her biological mother, she'd have said so.

"Shit," Kenny muttered. "It could also explain where the hell she's been. How she went from being front-page news during her father's election to disappearing completely. You think maybe her mother saw the scandals and got in touch?"

"That was my thought," Robert said tiredly. "Wouldn't be the first time an elected official's bought the silence of a 'less than suitable' woman."

"Must have been a hell of an offer for the woman to give up her kid, though."

"Yeah. And you've got to wonder if Brennan had his regrets about the deal when Addie nearly cost him the election. He could have lost his temper, spilled the truth . . ."

Kenny was silent for a long minute. "What's your plan?"

Robert shifted in his chair. "Stay the course. See if she mentions anything else."

Kenny's brown eyes flickered in disappointment.

"*If* she mentions something," Robert repeated. "I'm not going to dig."

"You going to tell her you know she's the governor's daughter?"

Robert's jaw tensed. "No."

"Come on, man."

"If she wants me to know, she'll tell me," Robert said. He said it not just to assuage his guilt but because he wanted it to be true. He barely knew the woman, and yet he had the strangest craving for her to trust him.

Kenny said nothing.

"What?" Robert snapped irritably.

"I know what Addie Blake looks like. I may be married, but I'm not blind."

Robert ground his teeth. "She doesn't look like that anymore."

"No? Better with age?"

Robert hesitated. "Different."

Kenny tilted his head back and laughed. "Oh my God. You've got a thing for her."

"I do not. I don't even . . . I *don't*," he insisted with a glare at the still-laughing Kenny. "It's as Martin put it: two birds, one stone. I get an event planner *and* the chance to get a scoop on Brennan."

"Yeah? And your event planner is going to just . . . open up? Tell you all of Daddy's secrets over crab cakes and chard?"

"No," Robert admitted. "In fact, I'm pretty sure I bungled it."

"Nah," Kenny said with a wave. "Bungle one of Martin's Machiavellian, exploit-whomever-whenever schemes? Impossible."

Chagrined, Robert shut his eyes and leaned his head back. "I tried to get her to talk about her past with exactly zero couth. All the walls went up. It's been a week and a half, and all I've gotten from her are daily email updates that read with as much personality as the reports we get every quarter on the state of the city's potholes."

"You don't like those? I always enjoy the suspense of not knowing which borough's going to win the award for the most," Kenny mused.

"What suspense? It's Queens," Robert muttered. "It's always Queens. The point is, she's avoiding me after I pushed too hard too fast."

"Shocking that she didn't want to let a practical stranger into her innermost thoughts. Though, in your defense, it's been a while since you've been on a proper date. To say that you're out of practice talking to women is a complete understatement."

Robert's eyes flew open. "I talk to women all the time."

"You talk to female voters all the time. There's a huge difference."

Robert glared at his friend. "Are you trying to tell me I don't have any moves?"

Kenny nodded. "Absolutely, man. You have *zero* moves."

"I don't need moves. I need an event planner."

"So find another event planner. One that has no connection to the governor, and one who doesn't make your dick twitch."

I want this one. And not for the reasons he should.

"Here's a question," Robert said slowly. "You don't want me to work with her because she's her father's daughter, but how is that any better than *not* giving her my business because of who her father is?"

Kenny hesitated. "Obnoxiously, I can see your point. If she's good at a job, she deserves a chance to do that job, regardless of her name. But doesn't she also deserve to know that you know who she really is?"

"That'll go over well. 'Hey, Adeline, just a quick heads-up: I know that prior to being a brunette event planner, you were a blonde who partied like it was your job, had nude photos plastered all over the internet, and did everything possible to destroy your dad's political career.'"

"Two sides to every story," Kenny pointed out. "Bet hers is a good one."

"Yeah. I just need to get her to tell me it."

"Oh, for sure," Kenny said with a nod. "I'm sure she's been practically dying for the right time to tell the mayor of New York City, her new celebrity client, all about her past."

Robert held his breath for a three-count and pressed his tongue hard against his bottom teeth. His chief of staff wasn't telling him anything he didn't already know, but it was annoying all the same. "I think I liked you better on vacation."

"This is why you pay me the big bucks. No, wait." Kenny snapped. "I make beans, because I'm a public servant *to* a public servant."

"You know full well I've offered a dozen times to hire you on as a consultant to my company and give the city-funded chief of staff title to someone else."

"Nope, I like being official. Almost as much as I like being your moral compass."

Robert rolled his eyes, but before he could tell Kenny where to shove his moral compass, there was a knock at the door. "Yeah," he called.

Darlene popped her head in. "Pardon the interruption, but Ms. Blake is here. She was hoping to take a look at the space for the party. Should I have one of the interns show her around?"

Kenny's eyebrows went up. "Well, well. Speak of the devil."

"Shut up, Kenny. And sure, Darlene. Get Ms. Blake whatever she needs."

Kenny stuck his tongue in his cheek as though physically refraining from comment. Then he turned toward Robert's assistant. "Actually, Darlene, show Ms. Blake in. I'd be happy to show her around."

Darlene was so accustomed to Kenny speaking on behalf of the mayor that she didn't even hesitate to do Kenny's bidding before Robert could stop the introduction.

A moment later, Adeline stepped through the doorway dressed in another of those damn blazers, a white blouse, and slacks. Perfectly respectable, and yet Robert couldn't shake the sense that they were all wrong for her.

Her blue eyes met his for only a moment, unreadable, before she looked over at Kenny, who was on his feet, a warm smile on his face. "Ms. Blake, I presume?"

She delivered a smooth smile alongside her handshake. "Yes. And you're Mr. Lamb."

"My fame precedes me, I see."

"Congratulations on your wedding. You were recently married, right? I did some research on all the key players," she said by way of explanation.

"Very recently married," Robert cut in. "In fact, I'm quite confident your bride would want you home for cocktail hour right about now, am I right, Kenny? For your staycation?"

"Oh, there's a pop-up flower stand I saw just around the corner," Adeline told Kenny. "I stopped to gawk at the gorgeous autumn bouquets. If your wife's at all a fall kind of gal, you'll earn major points if you pick one up on your way home."

"Are you kidding? The woman has more scarves and boots than I do underwear." He paused. "Too much info too soon?"

"Not at all," Adeline said with a bright smile. "I'm always happy when I can get on the fast track of friendship."

Since when? Robert had been busting his ass trying to get on the fast track of anything with her and had never gotten a smile half that bright.

"Bye, Kenny," Robert said pointedly.

Kenny didn't even look his way, but he took the hint, moving to the door even as he continued to chat up Adeline about *autumnal flowers*, of all things.

Finally, his chief of staff made it to the doorway, with the intent, Robert assumed, of telling Darlene to round up one of the interns after all.

Instead, Kenny shot them both a wide smile. "Enjoy Gracie Mansion, Ms. Blake. You won't find a better tour guide than the mayor himself."

Chapter Nine

"Kenny—"

His chief of staff was already out the door, closing it so that Robert couldn't summon Darlene without being blatantly rude.

Adeline gave Robert a knowing look. "You don't have to show me around. I should have called first, but I was in the neighborhood and hoped that your assistant could let me have a quick peek at the space without bugging you."

"I'll bet you did," he said, sitting back on his desk and crossing his arms over his chest.

Her eyes narrowed. "Meaning?"

"Meaning you've been avoiding me ever since our lunch."

"Or"—she snapped her fingers, as though just coming up with an alternative option—"I got all the information I needed from you in order to do my job at that lunch, and another face-to-face meeting hardly seemed necessary."

"That could be it," he granted, continuing to play the game. "*Or* I may have stomped where I had no business in our last conversation, and you've made me pay the price with the cold shoulder."

"See, now there you go again," she said softly. "The phrase *cold shoulder* is generally reserved for personal interactions. There's no such thing as a cold shoulder in a business relationship. Not if both parties are being professional. I've been in contact the proper amount to do my job."

His lips twitched in reluctant amusement. "Did you just call me unprofessional?"

"Did I?" She pretended to study her manicure, all innocence.

He laughed, and it was on the tip of his tongue to tell her she'd be a natural at politics, but he bit it back when he realized it was exactly the type of comment that would continue to push Adeline Blake further and further out of reach.

"At any rate, I owe you an apology," he said. "In truth, it's been a while since I've shared a meal with someone who wasn't actively trying to get something from me. Or from whom I didn't need something. Apparently I'm rusty on the art of conversation for conversation's sake."

"Apology accepted. Now if you'll excuse me, I really do need to see where—"

"Just one more thing," he said, reaching down to open his desk drawer. "I've actually got something I've been meaning to give you."

"Mr. Mayor, I really don't think—" She broke off when she saw what he was holding out to her, her clear irritation with him dissolving into amusement as she smiled. "A bottle of Excedrin?"

"I believe I've broken my assurances I'd be a no-pill kind of client." He rounded the desk and unceremoniously dropped the bottle into the open tote bag hooked over her shoulder. "Consider it an emergency stash. Now, about that tour."

Adeline sighed. "I'm not going to luck out and get a twenty-two-year-old intern to show me around, am I?"

"That would be luck?"

She grinned. "Well, to be honest, I was hoping that a newbie wouldn't know all of the nuances of past parties, in which case I could be free to view the space as a blank canvas."

"Compromise," he proposed. "I'll show you the general space where I like to host, but I promise not to say a word about what Jada's done in the past."

She shifted slightly, clearly bothered. "Why? Don't get me wrong, I respect the whole get-your-hands-dirty personal approach, but you can't tell me that the mayor of New York City doesn't have something better to do with his time." Her voice was steady, and politely challenging, but the wariness in her gaze told him something else. Not of an event planner impatient with a client's stubbornness. Not even a governor's daughter, jaded by the world of politics. But of a woman who didn't trust men—who didn't trust *him*.

The realization sent a quiet anger through him, but it had a silver lining. He now knew exactly where he'd gone wrong with Adeline Blake.

"Can I be honest?" he asked, tempering his usual full smile to reflect how he really felt: nearly as wary as her.

She shrugged. "Of course."

"I told you the other day that I liked that you didn't tolerate my crap, and I meant it. I don't often interact with people who don't want something from me—or who I'm not trying to, uh, shall we say curry favor with."

"Understandable," Adeline said. "Part of the job."

"It is. But even when I'm not in mayor mode . . . I am. Or rather, people see me that way. At the risk of sounding very *poor famous dude*, it's rare that people treat me like a regular guy."

She pursed her lips, then nodded. "Sure, I can see that. What's that have to do with me and the event I'm planning?"

He grinned. "Well, see, you're sort of proving my point. You don't mince your words around me. You don't get flustered. Hell, I'm not even entirely sure you don't dislike me." The fact that she didn't rush to contradict him was hardly reassuring, but Robert pushed forward. "The fact is, Ms. Blake . . . you're rather refreshing."

She lifted her eyebrows. "You like me because I don't like you?"

"Basically," Robert said, lifting his shoulders. "Maybe it's my corrupt politician's soul that can't help but want to win you over, or maybe I just enjoy being treated like a man instead of a title, but I enjoy your company. And at the risk of sounding like an awkward schoolboy, I thought it might be nice if you and I could become friends."

The moment the words were out of his mouth, he realized they had nothing to do with his desire to learn what she knew about her father. While the aspiring governor in him still wanted to prove to the world he was a better man, and would make a better governor, than George Brennan, he couldn't pretend that he looked at Adeline and thought of the governor.

Because when he looked at Adeline, he didn't think of himself as the mayor. Somehow he'd turned into a goddamn Hugh Grant movie, standing in front of a girl, asking her to like him.

Because he meant what he'd said. *He* liked *her*. He liked the way she made him feel. Women tended to act fluttery around him, and it had gotten even worse after the Man of the Year debacle. For that matter, Robert had a hard time figuring out who his true friends were. Other than Kenny, who had no problem giving it to Robert straight, everyone else seemed to see him as Mr. Mayor first, Robert second.

He craved something different. Damn it, he just wanted a friend. Granted, his body still wanted a lot more from Adeline Blake. But he'd settle for someone to talk to.

"Friends," she said skeptically.

"I make a good one," he said, spreading his hands to the side. "For example, if you ever need a ride to the airport, I have my driver on speed dial. And if you need someone to help you move . . . I know a guy."

She laughed. "A good friend to have, indeed." Adeline looked him over for a moment, then sighed. "Fine. Show me your party space."

"And then we can become best friends?" he joked, opening the door for her.

"Depends. Does your driver go to LaGuardia *and* JFK?"

"For my friends, he'll even go to Jersey if you need to fly out of Newark."

She made an impressed noise. "You make a compelling case, Mr. Mayor."

"Think on it, Ms. Blake. Who knows, you may even get around to calling me Robert one of these days."

"Let's not start talking crazy. Now, tell me about your home," she said, looking around as they left the office space. "It's beautiful."

"I can't take much credit. It was built in 1799 near the same site where George Washington commandeered a building during the American Revolution because of its strategic proximity to Hell Gate."

She shook her head questioningly.

"A strait of the East River, and potential attack point for the British fleets. In fact, the British destroyed the house that Washington had built. Archibald Gracie had this one built later, named after him, obviously. It's served various purposes over the years. A home, a museum, a classroom. It even served as the public restroom and ice-cream stand for Carl Schurz Park in the early 1900s."

"Really?" She sounded genuinely interested. "When did it become the official mayor's residence?"

"In 1942, though not all mayors have opted to live here. For example, Bloomberg held meetings and private events in the mansion but didn't actually live here. Though he did foot the bill for a major renovation, which brings us full circle to the start of this tangent: I can't take much credit for anything in the house. It looks the same now as when I moved in."

"No urge to put your mark on it?" she asked, as they stepped into one of the parlors.

"If it needed maintenance or restoration, then absolutely. But cosmetic changes for the sake of it? Nah. Feels a bit like a dog peeing on a fence post just to say, 'I was here.' I'd rather leave my legacy with my policy—be remembered for the good I did, not the throw pillows I've selected."

"Ah, so then you'd hover around an interior designer as much as you do your event planner?" she asked with a smile, jotting something in her notebook as she took in the room.

Only if she looked like you.

It wasn't just Adeline's looks, though. Something about this woman's presence both calmed and ignited him. Highly annoying, considering she rarely called him anything other than *Mr. Mayor*.

"Why do I get the feeling I look like a control freak through your eyes?" he said, slightly dodging her question.

"It's not always a bad thing," she said almost distractedly, continuing to take notes.

"Could that have been . . . a compliment?" he said, lowering his voice to a teasing whisper.

Her lips tilted in a womanly smile. "If I ever compliment you, you'll know."

"*If.* Ouch."

"Don't worry," she said breezily. "You strike me as a man who enjoys a challenge."

That I do, Ms. Blake. That I do, he thought, his eyes drifting over her curves when she turned to study the rest of the space.

"So, this is all fair game for the party?" she asked, oblivious to his thoughts as she wandered into another room. "One hundred and fifty people is a lot for a private residence, even if it is technically a mansion."

"The whole first floor, minus my private office," he said, following her into the adjoining room. "Basically, if it's on the school field trip tour, it's fair game for guests."

"Got it." She continued jotting notes as she roamed around his home.

The mansion was good-sized, but because it was old, it lacked the open floor plan of more modern homes, with much of the first floor taken up by a bunch of smaller spaces. There was, however, a decent-sized ballroom, which was usually the focal point of any gathering. Something Adeline had realized all on her own, apparently, as she was spending more time in the iconic blue room than the others.

She set her notebook on a small end table and switched to her phone, using it to take a video of the space. "What's upstairs?" she asked distractedly, spinning in a slow circle to get a 360-degree view of the room with her camera.

"What?" he asked, realizing he was watching her with a bit more intensity than a mayor should have when looking at an event planner.

"You said everything on the first floor except your office is accessible to guests. What's upstairs?"

"The living quarters." He hesitated, not wanting to have a repeat of their lunch date when he'd pushed too hard and scared her off, then decided to go for it. "Want to see?"

She gave him a startled look, then narrowed her eyes just slightly. "Depends. Will I regret it?"

Robert grinned. "I'm willing to risk it if you are."

Chapter Ten

Tuesday, October 13

A month ago, Adeline would have sworn she'd never set foot into a politician's world. She'd had plenty of firsthand experience with the formal, uptight, manufactured life of a first family, and to say the memories were unpleasant was a massive understatement.

And yet here she was, not only planning a party for an elected official but touring his private quarters, seeing where he lived, how he lived. Most baffling of all, she was enjoying it. Enjoying *him*, she realized as she cast a sidelong glance at the mayor.

He'd excused himself a couple of minutes earlier to take a phone call, and instead of it feeling rude, she liked that he knew she wouldn't get all huffy at the fact that the most powerful man in the city might possibly have something more pressing than making small talk with her. It was hard to explain, even to herself, but she felt a strange sense of pleasure that he seemed to think of her as a part of his inner circle, rather than an exception to it.

But along with that pleasure came a vague sense of foreboding, the same trepidation that had her keeping her distance the past week. He'd been absolutely right in gently accusing her of avoiding him. On a professional level, she'd been perfectly thorough. She'd never let the event she'd been hired for suffer simply because the client made her nervous.

And he *did* make her nervous. Their disastrous conversation over lunch had made her realize just how much damage this man could do if he ever found out who she really was. And her alarm hadn't come so much from the fact that he'd clearly been trying to learn more about her, but from the fact that for an insane moment, she'd wanted to tell him.

Maintaining her privacy was precisely the reason she didn't date and made a point of steering clear of men she found attractive, and for all his insistence that that lunch had been a work meeting and her desperation to believe it, she knew there'd been something simmering between them that went beyond bland discussions about dress code and appetizers.

When she was around him, she kept forgetting herself. She kept forgetting she was the daughter of his political rival, and even more puzzling, she even forgot she was an event planner. She was simply a woman who enjoyed a man, who felt both breathless and safe when she was near him.

It was this strange dichotomy of emotion the mayor brought out in her that had her pulling back. The old version of herself had trusted easily and believed the good in people. Strange, perhaps, given the fact that she was raised by an unscrupulous bastard like George Brennan. Or perhaps it was *because* her father had been such a corrupt snake that she'd needed to believe he was the exception, rather than the rule.

Her younger self had given her heart away easily, confided in people she shouldn't have, trusted those who said, "No, *of course* the drink wasn't that strong," and assured her that the photos were for "their eyes only." She'd believed men who'd said they'd call the next day.

The result? She'd had far too many hazy nights where she couldn't remember the details, the entire internet had seen her boobs, and she'd yet to meet a man who thought she was worth sticking by when things got even a little bit complicated. For that matter, she'd spent way too many hours blinking back tears when she realized the guy who'd said all the right things on Saturday was completely out of her life by Sunday.

Yes, all of her acting out had been on her agenda, or so she'd thought, but she couldn't deny that there'd been plenty of hungover mornings in her early twenties when she'd wished someone would have seen her behavior for what it was—desperation.

A longing for someone to *care*.

She'd grown up since then. Knew that it was better to keep the deepest parts of herself protected. Thus, she wasn't in the market for any kind of romantic entanglement, especially with the freaking mayor of New York City.

But. His suggestion of being friends . . .

That held a surprising amount of appeal.

Other than Jane, Rosalie, and her coworkers, friends were something Adeline had been a little short on since moving back to New York. Part of it was just the nature of building a new business from the ground up, but she couldn't place all the blame on her long work hours. Addie's innate friendliness was forever battling with Adeline's reluctance to trust people, which applied to all aspects of her social life, not just romance.

And while Robert Davenport the mayor was hardly the best person to befriend, Robert Davenport the man was awfully easy to be around.

He was still on the phone, so she wandered around his living room. It was a little too museum-esque for her tastes, but it was impressive in a stately, old-fashioned kind of way. Her father would have loved it.

She picked up a framed photograph, her heart giving a little squeeze when she saw it was of Robert and his parents at Disney World. The mayor looked to be ten or so. She smiled a little at the happy faces and the mouse ears, the normalcy of the moment catching her by surprise. From what she knew about Robert Davenport Sr., he'd already been entrenched in local politics by the time the current mayor was in elementary school, and yet he'd still taken the time for a family vacation.

To be fair, her father had taken the occasional getaway as well. Just not with her. George Brennan had been fond of "getting off the grid," as he'd called it, which, as Addie had gotten older, she had realized was his way of sleeping with women half his age—married women, multiple women . . .

He'd quietly drive off in the early morning to a rented house in the Catskills, or wherever, and come back days later a little more smiley, a little more smug.

When she'd been really young—far younger than Robert in this picture—she'd cried to her nanny about his desertion, wondering why he didn't take her along. Wondering why she didn't get to go on weekend getaways to Cape Cod like her friends.

It hadn't taken long until she'd changed her tune entirely. Eventually, she'd come to eagerly relish seeing his taillights, rejoicing in the break from his oppressive, controlling presence.

The mayor came up behind her, interrupting her bitter memories. "You'd never know it from my face, but that photo was taken about five minutes before a full-fledged breakdown."

Adeline turned toward him, picture frame still in her hand. "You? Anything less than a model specimen of humanity?"

"I know. I find it shocking, too," he said with a smile, though his eyes were a little sad as he looked down at the three grinning faces. "I'm all smiles in that moment, but fast-forward a few seconds to when they told me it was time to go get dinner so we could be back in time for the fireworks show. It didn't at all gel with my plan of having a churro for 'dinner' while waiting in line to go on Space Mountain for the third time that day."

"A roller coaster after churros? You were a brave kid."

"I was a spoiled brat," he said with a small smile.

She glanced up at his classically handsome profile, at the conservative blue suit. Even after hours, his tie knot was impeccable, and there wasn't a wrinkle in sight. He looked like the type of kid who would have ironed his own polo shirts and polished his own loafers.

Adeline told him so as she set the photo back on the shelf.

The mayor laughed. "Hardly. My knees were always skinned. I was forever in trouble for not going to bed when I was told, for trying to maneuver more TV time than I was allowed. I refused to eat vegetables, I got in trouble in school, and I spent all of fifth grade with *damn* as my favorite word."

She laughed along with him at the mental image he'd described. "You're so straitlaced now. What happened?"

Even before his eyes dimmed, she regretted the question. She knew exactly what had happened. The whole country did.

He reached out and straightened the picture frame, though it didn't need straightening. "Everything changed when he died. I guess that's an obvious statement. Of course things changed. But I sometimes think I became a different person that day. I *chose* to be a different person. The day after the funeral, I made myself a promise to honor him. To do everything exactly right to carry on the legacy that he'd started. To do our family's name proud because he no longer could."

"He'd be proud of you," Adeline said quietly.

Robert's smile was sad. "Yeah. But the hell of it is, I think he'd have been proud of me even if I'd kept on being a terror. He always told me it wasn't the type of person you were on paper that mattered—it was the way you made other people feel that was important. He told me I could be an A-plus student and a grade-A jerk, a struggling student who spread good in the world, or anything in between. My choice."

The difference between their fathers was so stark she almost laughed. Her father's "pep talks" had been more in the vein of: *Jesus, Addie, a B-plus in social studies? For God's sake, your teacher knows who I am—how do you think that looks?*

She swallowed against the memories of a childhood that had been pretty much the opposite of what the mayor was describing. "Your dad sounds pretty amazing."

"Yeah. He was. My mom's really great, too. I know it's a cliché, but she really stepped in and played the role of both parents as best she could. She always fulfilled her promises to practice soccer with me in Central Park, even when she forgot to bring a change of shoes after her workday. Truth be told, it was a little embarrassing to have my mom running around the park in stilettos, but I never let her know it. And now, I'm grateful."

"You should be. You were lucky." She winced. "God. I didn't mean lucky that your dad—"

"No, I was lucky," he interrupted, kindly smoothing over her faux pas. "He died too young, and I hate that, but I sometimes think I'd rather have had a dad like him for a few years than a jerk who keeps on keeping on."

Her shoulders tensed, and for a moment her heart stopped, thinking it was a repeat of their lunch, when he'd mentioned her "dark secrets." But a quick glance showed that he was looking out the window, distracted, his statement not pointed to her specifically.

She relaxed. Even felt brave enough to respond. "I think you're right," she said softly.

He glanced at her, his gaze curious but not prying. "About?"

She fiddled with the button on her sleeve. "That having a great father for a few years is better than having a crappy one for a lifetime."

"Speaking from experience?" His tone was nonchalant, one new friend getting to know another, and she bit her lip, taking an emotional step forward in the name of being a functional human being who didn't let her father and her past rule every action.

Adeline glanced up at him with a small smile. "Yeah. My father was—oh, how do I put this?—an asshole."

"Was?"

"Is," she amended. "He's still alive, just not a part of my life."

"I'm sorry," he said softly. "That must be difficult. Especially after losing your mother."

"Not really," she said. "I mean, yes, Mom's passing was gut-wrenching. But I don't miss my father."

"Did you have a falling-out?"

Abruptly, she remembered who she was talking to. He was quite possibly the worst person in whom to confide the gritty details of her family life. "Something like that. Anyway. I should let you get back to your evening. Thanks for the tour. I doubt I'll be acquainted with the next mayor, so this was likely a once-in-a-lifetime opportunity."

The mayor studied her for a long minute, then, instead of saying goodbye and showing her to the door, surprised her by shrugging out of his suit jacket and tossing it over the back of a chair. "You like pizza?"

"I—What?"

"Pizza. Carbs. Cheese. Greasy meat optional."

"I'm familiar."

The mayor's fingers flicked open the buttons at his cuff, and he began rolling up the crisp white sleeves. "But are you a fan?"

"Sure. Who doesn't like pizza?" she replied, trying not to get distracted by the slow reveal of his muscular forearms.

"I'm an Italian sausage and mushroom kind of guy, but I can be talked into just about anything."

"Is this your way of telling me I should cancel the caterers I've already booked for the party and just see if Grimaldi's delivers?"

"Can't say I'm not intrigued by that idea, but I was thinking more for tonight."

"Ah. Well, in that case, have at it and enjoy."

He scratched his cheek. "I can't figure out if you're being deliberately obtuse or if my game is really that stale."

"Your *friend* game, you mean?"

He grinned. "Yeah. That."

She sucked in her cheeks and considered the invitation, because no, she wasn't that obtuse, and his game wasn't that bad. She knew an invitation when she heard one.

The question was, did she want to accept it?

"No mushrooms," she said finally.

"You're killin' me, Blake," he said, but she definitely saw the victorious tilt of his smile as he pulled out his cell phone. "I'll get us some wine," he said, still looking at his phone and heading to the kitchen. "Make yourself at home."

She glanced down at her blazer, knowing that if she were really at home, she'd have shed the dreaded garment ten minutes ago. For an annoying moment, it was tempting . . .

Instead, she sat, blazer still in place, acting as a shield. Addie might be choosing the music, but Adeline was still very much driving the car.

Chapter Eleven

"I just need to be sure . . . am I going crazy? I am, right? Our girl's not seriously telling us she had dinner with the mayor," Rosalie said, turning to Jane.

"You're not the crazy one—*she* is," Jane said, emphatically pointing at Adeline.

Adeline nibbled on the corner of a chip. "It's really not the big deal you two are making it out to be. It was just dinner. Pizza."

"That's even worse!" Jane said shrilly. "It's so intimate."

Adeline glanced over at her calmer friend. "Please tell her there's nothing intimate about Italian sausage." She winced as she caught herself. "Yeah, I heard it."

"It is a little out of character," Rosalie said slowly. "You haven't exactly made it a secret how you feel about men these days. To say nothing of your thoughts on elected officials."

"I didn't sleep with the guy, we just had pizza."

"I'd actually be less concerned if you'd slept with him," Rosalie admitted.

"*Agreed,*" Jane said, smacking the table. "A sexy fling with the Man of the Year is one thing. A cozy dinner at his place is just . . ." She threw her hands up. "I can't. I literally can't process it."

"You don't have to process anything," Adeline said, dunking the chip into the salsa and stuffing the whole thing in her mouth. "It was a onetime thing. The party's next weekend, and then I'll probably never see him again."

"What if he wants you to be his forever event planner?"

"He won't. His regular planner's one of the best in the city, and I'm sure she'll be back from maternity leave by the time he needs to hire someone again."

"Is his regular event planner hot and single?" Jane pointed out.

"She's married."

"Exactly. Much less susceptible to his sexy face than single you."

Adeline sighed and looked again to the perpetually calm Rosalie. "Make it stop."

"Just promise you'll warn us if you start to fall for the guy," her friend said, fiddling with her chip. "Much as I love the idea of you landing the hottest guy in the city, I also know just how tricky that would be for you."

"Tricky is an understatement, given he's likely running against The Bastard in the next election," she said, knowing that both of her long-time friends knew she was referring to the father she'd all but disowned.

Adeline hadn't known Rosalie as long as she'd known Jane, but they still went all the way back to high school. Adeline had been the loose cannon, Jane the genius, and Rosalie had been, well . . . *perfect*.

For starters, she was gorgeous. Her mother was Indian, her father French, and the combination was the dazzling Rosalie and her equally attractive twin brother. She'd also been an honor roll student, captain of the soccer and golf teams, student body president, and debate team superstar.

But where Rosalie really shone was her kindness. She'd had her pick of the Ivy Leagues and had chosen Cornell because it was an easy drive back to her parents' home just outside Albany after her mom was diagnosed with MS. She'd also been just about the only person in their prep school who'd gone out of her way to be kind to the new girl.

The mid-to-late teen years were hard enough without being the daughter of the newly elected governor, who took every opportunity to belittle and berate her. The last thing Addie had needed on the heels of a new home and new public responsibilities as New York's first daughter had been a new school to boot, but her father hadn't even pretended to listen to Addie's pleas to finish out high school with her friends.

In hindsight, Adeline probably couldn't even blame the other kids at the prep school for keeping their distance from the moody, volatile Addie, but it also made her all the more grateful that Rosalie had seen through the tough-girl act and had gone out of her way not just to be nice, but to befriend her.

Eventually, Addie had introduced Rosalie to Jane, who'd still been attending the public school in their neighborhood, and somehow, despite being extremely different personalities, they'd all become friends.

They'd stayed in touch and remained close even after Jane and Rosalie had gone off to different colleges, and Addie had begun what she liked to think of as the reign of terror that was her late teens and early twenties. Even after Rosalie had been in Texas for years as a marketing director at an Austin start-up. Even when Addie all but dropped off the grid after discovering her mother was still alive.

"You know," Adeline said, looking thoughtfully at Rosalie over the top of her margarita, "I actually thought about setting you and the mayor up."

"Wait, what?" Rosalie's eyes went wide.

"You said yourself he was hot," Adeline pointed out. "You're also beautiful, well spoken, polished. You never look bad in a photograph, and you never say the wrong thing. I literally can't think of a more perfect future First Lady of New York."

"Oooh, I *see* that!" Jane said, pivoting in her chair to stare at Rosalie.

Adeline gave Jane an exasperated expression. "You were *just* warning me off of the guy."

"Warning *you* off, yes. But Rosalie . . ."

Adeline tried to ignore the sting. It wasn't as if Jane were saying anything Adeline herself hadn't thought. Even if she were inclined to pursue the mayor, and she wasn't, she knew that she was the last thing someone like him needed. Her past alone made her an inconceivable choice for him, and even if she could keep her past mistakes under wraps, she would never be the right woman for him. She may have mastered the bun and the blazers, but she was still the woman who collected adventurous lingerie and loved tequila.

"The guy's definitely attractive," Rosalie said. "But I don't know that I want one of Adeline's rejects," she said with a smile intended to annoy Adeline.

"I wouldn't let that stop me," Jane said, fanning herself. "If it weren't for Dan . . . Too bad I love that man so damn much. Seriously, Rosalie, let Adeline fix you up, so I can live vicariously."

"Hello," Rosalie said, staring at the admittedly, occasionally tone-deaf Jane. "Are you not seeing what I'm seeing?" She pointed at Adeline.

Jane glanced over and narrowed her eyes.

"Ever since she came back from New Mexico with her hair brown, she's been like this buttoned-up ice woman. But when she talks about *him* . . ." Rosalie made an unrecognizable hissing, clicking noise.

"What was that?" Jane asked.

"Fire igniting," Rosalie explained. "Whatever, so sound effects and act-outs aren't my strong suit. The point is—"

"If I sound fiery when I talk about the mayor, it's only because he's a control freak and pain in the ass," Adeline interjected. "The man doesn't know how to delegate, is hell-bent on carrying on his father's legacy without ever checking in with himself, and . . ."

Adeline's thoughts scattered a little as she realized she wasn't being entirely fair to the mayor. Yes, he was obsessed with his image, as a man in his position had to be. But he could also be funny and irreverent. He could also be spontaneous and casual.

He'd proven that yesterday, first with the tour of his home, then the invitation of dinner. Even the way he ate pizza was appealing, somehow both buttoned-up precise and outright relishing, all at the same time.

"Do we need more margaritas before we get back to the *real* elephant in the room?" Jane asked, oblivious to Adeline's conflicted emotions.

"What, the fact that the mayor's very likely running against my father in the next election?"

"He told you that?"

"No," Adeline said slowly. "He's never confirmed it. But there are the rumors . . ."

"You could ask him," Rosalie nudged.

Adeline snorted. "How? 'Hey, by the way, I'm just curious, are you trying to boot my asshole father from his job next year?'"

"Your dad *is* an asshole," Jane muttered. "The man hid the existence of your mother from you, never appreciated how amazing you were, and turned you into this." Jane waved at her.

"Hey!" Adeline said, truly stung.

The often too-blunt Jane was instantly contrite, and she reached out to squeeze Adeline's hand. "Don't get me wrong. You are of course allowed to change, and I love everything that Adeline is and that Adeline's built. But I miss Addie."

"I'm still her."

"You're wearing a blazer," Rosalie pointed out.

"Because I came from work. And under the blazer is all party," Adeline said in a mock whisper, pulling out the conservative gray blazer on one side to show the lacy hot pink camisole beneath it.

"Snore. It doesn't count when you cover it up," Rosalie said, the steel in her voice belying the playful *I dare you* twinkle in her eye and providing a glimpse at just why she'd been so effective on her high school debate team. "Prove Addie's still in there."

"What, you want to see my blonde roots?" Adeline asked, already lifting her hands to her hair, and dipping her head slightly.

"No, who cares about your hair?" Rosalie said. "I want to see Addie's spirit. I want to see the girl who loved to dance."

Adeline laughed. "Oh God. No."

"She *does* still love to dance," Jane said, jumping on the bandwagon. "I've seen it."

"Yeah, in the privacy of my apartment." *Where there are no cameras, and no judgment.*

"There have got to be like a dozen clubs around here, right?" Rosalie said, pulling out her phone. "Even on a Wednesday?"

"Yes!" Jane said, tapping her fingers on the table. "Party on a school night, I love it. Somebody make sure I drink plenty of water, and I'm in."

"*Not* in. You guys are insane," Adeline said, even as she felt her old self start to stir at the prospect. "I have an early client coffee meeting tomorrow, and then later, the date you tricked me into by telling me it was a networking meeting." She shot Jane a glare.

"Ooh, tell!" Rosalie perked up.

"There's this guy at work who's perfect for her," Jane said. "She kept saying no, so I told him that she was excited to meet him and was free tomorrow at seven."

"So, a flat-out lie," Rosalie said.

Jane nodded, then slapped Rosalie's palm, which she'd lifted for a high five.

Adeline glared at both of them. To say she was dreading the date was an understatement, though she had to admit that maybe it wasn't the worst idea. Maybe a romantic endeavor would help her stop thinking about whatever strange tension was brewing between her and the mayor, which she wasn't entirely sure wasn't overprotective Jane's plan in the first place.

"Okay, so back to dancing—"

"Nope," Adeline said. "I've already been maneuvered into a first date tomorrow. I'm not going to get talked into dancing, too."

Both of her friends just looked at her, as though waiting for her to realize that . . .

She wanted to go dancing.

Adeline bit her lip. "Okay, let's do it."

"Yay, Addie's back!" Jane said happily.

"Just for tonight," Adeline said with a small smile, even as she felt herself relax in a way she hadn't in months.

"I'll take it," Rosalie said with a smile. "Just one more thing . . ."

"What?"

Her friends spoke at the exact same time. "Lose the blazer."

Chapter Twelve

Thursday, October 15

"Late night?"

Adeline heaved her head out of her hand and looked up to see Robert Davenport lounging idly in the doorway of her office. "What the—How did you get in here?"

"Door?" he said, crossing his arms and tilting his head as he studied her.

"It's barely seven thirty. My team's not even here yet."

"Exactly. No gatekeeper made it that much easier."

"Isn't the downstairs door locked? Never mind—" she said tiredly. "I forget who I'm dealing with. It'd take more than a locked door to keep the mayor from getting where he wants to go."

She opened her desk drawer and pulled out a bottle of Excedrin. Not the one he'd given her as a joke. She'd set that one aside, and she had the unnerving suspicion that she'd be holding on to that bottle for a long time to come like some sort of sentimental souvenir.

Ugh. What was this man turning her into?

She put two fingers to the throb in her temple. The coffee she'd had during her seven o'clock meeting had taken the edge off the initial ache, but not erased it completely.

"Ah, so you *did* need pills," he said softly, pointing at the painkillers.

"Apparently, though surprisingly, not because of you," she said, dumping two white capsules into her palm and washing them down with water. She let out a groan when he ambled all the way into her office and plopped into the chair across from her. "*Surely* you have somewhere else to be. Ribbons to cut, medals to award?"

He gave a slow smile. "You're extra sharp when you're hungover. I quite like it."

"I'm not hungover," she muttered.

"No?"

"Just a little . . . tired."

Going to bed at three a.m. would do that to you. Though the tequila hadn't helped, either. Compared to her old ways, her alcohol consumption had been *extremely* moderate, but there had been some imbibing, and her body was not so gently reminding her she wasn't twenty-three anymore.

On a normal day, she could handle it. But seeing him first thing was not a normal day, and she could barely handle the man sitting across from her when she was at her best. With a fuzzy head and carb craving?

She'd need to watch her step.

"So," he said, his tone casual, "what inspired the nighttime festivities? Hot date?"

"No, that's tonight," she said distractedly, checking an email that had just come up on her computer screen.

"You have a date tonight?" The sharpness in his tone got her attention, and she glanced across the desk to find him looking stormy.

"My friend set me up with a colleague. Is that a problem?"

His jaw tensed. "Of course not. For some reason, I didn't realize you were on the dating market."

A telling statement that gave her a little thrill, as did the slightly competitive light in his eyes.

And what if you'd known I had been on the dating market? Then what?

She didn't ask it. Obviously. She wasn't for him, and he wasn't for her. Not now, not ever.

Adeline gave an impartial smile. "Honestly, I didn't realize I was on the market, either, but you'd understand if you knew my friend Jane. She's sort of a force of nature when she latches on to an idea, and she apparently thinks this guy is my soul mate." Sighing with dread at the upcoming date, Adeline dug her fingers into her hair and massaged her scalp lightly. "God, I would kill for an egg-and-cheese sandwich. With bacon. Doesn't bacon sound good?"

He pointed a finger at her water bottle. "Drink that."

"Yes, sir." She did as instructed, glaring at him as she took three big gulps, as though this were his fault. "I bet you're *never* hungover."

"It's been a while," he admitted, after a slight pause.

She only managed a grunt in response.

"Did you at least have fun?" he asked.

Adeline smiled in spite of the headache, remembering how free and happy she'd felt dancing the night away with her two best friends. "I did."

"Well then." He shrugged. "Sometimes that's all that matters."

Her smile turned grim. "Would you still say that to someone if they'd been out on the dance floor at three a.m. on a Wednesday night?"

He hesitated again, only for the briefest of moments, but it was there. "I'll admit that those of us in the public spotlight do tend to live by slightly different standards."

Didn't she know it. *Damn it, Addie, I understand you don't care about embarrassing yourself, but it's past time you started caring that your childish antics embarrass me.*

"Well," she said, crossing her legs and pivoting her chair more fully toward him. "If you ever want to let me set you up with my friend . . ."

She didn't tell him that Rosalie had stayed out just as late as Adeline last night, though her dancing had been decidedly more restrained, due more to a lack of rhythm than anything else. Rosalie was an all-star in all things except dancing, but Adeline was reasonably sure that twerking wasn't on Robert Davenport's list of "must haves" in a wife.

He stared at her with an unreadable expression. "I'll think on it. Where are you going on your date?"

"Why?" she asked warily.

He leaned back in his chair and stayed silent.

Her head was hurting just enough for her to acquiesce. "I can't remember the name of the restaurant off the top of my head, and no, I'm not going to look it up, but it's a little Italian place in the East Village."

"The East Village?" he said, frowning.

"I can draw you a map, if you'd like."

He ignored the sarcasm. "If you want good Italian, you should go to this little hole in the wall over—"

"No," she interrupted. "No, thank you. The place my date picked gets great reviews, and it's close to my apartment, so win-win."

He narrowed his eyes. "Do you think that's why he picked it? In hopes of going back to your apartment after dinner?"

Adeline let out a surprised laugh. "Mr. Mayor."

He looked properly chagrined. "I apologize. I overstepped. Can I claim concerned friend?"

She tried to hide her smile, refusing to be charmed, and failed. "Sure. Forgiven. And for what it's worth, I think he picked it because it's near the jazz club he's taking me to."

"You like jazz?"

She shrugged. "Guess I'll find out."

"What sort of music do you usually like?"

"Everything. Miley Cyrus. Bruce Springsteen. ABBA. I got into country music the past couple years and still listen to that sometimes. If I had to pick what I listen to most, I'm pretty obsessed with Michael Jackson."

He grinned. "Fun fact: I know the 'Thriller' dance."

She lifted an eyebrow. "*That* wasn't in *Citizen* magazine."

"A man's got to have some secrets from the public, Ms. Blake."

Adeline had the sudden urge to know them all—to know this man beyond the magazine covers and the interviews. She took another sip of water. "So, at what point do you tell me why you're at my office so early?"

"Ah. Right. I came to talk about the party."

"Really. Remind me to tell you about this newfangled concept called email one of these days. It's pretty handy once you get the hang of it."

He ignored her. "I'd like you to come to the party."

"Well, yeah." She placed the lid back on her water bottle. "That's sort of in the job description."

"I don't mean behind the scenes. I mean as a guest. No hiding out in the kitchens wearing an ugly uniform."

"What?" Her fuzzy thoughts scrambled even further. "I can't. *No.* Why would I do that? Also, why would you assume the uniform would be ugly?"

She didn't think it was her imagination that his gaze dropped to her ever-present blazer just for a second, as though saying, *that's why.*

"If it makes you feel better, I asked the same of Jada," he said. "Who better to know how a party is going than someone *at* the party?"

"I *will* be at the party. Just as an employee."

He was already shaking his head. "I want you there experiencing it as a guest. You'll get a better sense if they hate the caviar or the band if you're mingling."

"But—"

"I'm afraid I insist, Ms. Blake."

She looked up in surprise as he stood. "You're leaving?"

The mayor's smile was wide and cocky. "Is that disappointment I hear in your voice?"

"Hardly. I'm just trying to figure out how to deal with a man who's used to getting his way."

He rebuttoned his suit jacket and adjusted his tie, seeming to switch between man and mayor right before her eyes. "Have a pleasant day, Ms. Blake, and enjoy your date this evening."

"I will," she said, hearing the flatness of her tone, chagrined to realize that he was exactly right. There was disappointment in her voice, when, if she were smart, she should be relieved.

He pointed once more to the water bottle on her desk. "Drink that."

"You could have bossed me around via email, you know!" she called after his retreating back.

He was gone.

She picked up the water again and sipped it.

What had *that* been about? She didn't buy for one second that it had just been about his insistence she attend the party as a guest. Nor did she entirely buy that his motives for asking were as pure as he'd claimed. She'd planned plenty of events, and this marked the first time a client had made a point of insisting she mingle with guests rather than hide behind the scenes.

Then again, the mayor was hardly typical in his approach to party planning, and she'd believed him when he'd said he'd asked the same of his previous event planner.

But the request absolutely had not necessitated an in-person drop-by.

The prospect that he'd stopped by today simply because he wanted to see her both thrilled and terrified her.

Almost as much as it terrified her how much she'd wanted to see him.

Annoyed at the thought, she crumpled the plastic water bottle and shoved it with more force than necessary into the recycling bin. She forced her attention back to work and managed to clear a bunch of emails out of her in-box before the second interruption of her morning.

Cordelia entered her office with a paper bag. "Good morning! Your breakfast delivery just got here."

"Oh, thank God," Adeline said, pushing some files out of the way to make room to eat at her desk. "You read my mind."

Her assistant blinked. "I didn't order it. I thought you did."

Adeline shook her head, disappointed. "They must have delivered to the wrong address."

"Nope, it has your name on it," Cordelia said, reading the receipt stapled to the bag. "Bacon, egg, and cheese breakfast sandwich, extra bacon, and a bottled water."

Adeline felt a little breathless. She'd never realized until now that a greasy breakfast sandwich could be . . . romantic.

"Oh. Yeah, that is mine after all."

"So you *did* order it?" Cordelia said, sounding understandably confused as she handed over the bag.

"No," Adeline said with a little smile. "But I know who did."

Chapter Thirteen

At six o'clock the night of the mayor's party, Adeline tucked a loose strand of hair behind her ear and finally, *finally*, allowed herself to take a deep breath and stop moving for the first time all day.

Taking a look around the first floor of Gracie Mansion, she couldn't stop the grin from spreading over her face. Her back hurt, she hadn't eaten since breakfast, and she didn't even want to see a mirror, but she was also thrilled that the effort had paid off.

She only hoped the mayor would be as well. She'd know soon enough.

Adeline winced as she glanced at her watch. She'd know *really* soon.

She spotted Luciana in the corner of the ballroom, explaining something to the lead singer of the band, and headed that way. Usually Adeline managed events on her own, but for larger, more high-profile events, they sometimes doubled up. She was especially glad to have her junior event planner at this one, given the mayor's request that she mingle as a guest. It would be easier to do so knowing Luciana was behind the scenes, managing the caterer and waitstaff.

She didn't *hate* the mayor's suggestion of mingling with the guests. On a personal level, the thought of having to rub elbows with the political elite was her nightmare. But professionally, she could see the merit. It would be easier to gauge how the party was going if she was on the front lines.

Still, it didn't mean she was excited about the prospect of the strapless bra and constricting dress that awaited her when all she wanted was to blend into the background.

Luciana smiled as Adeline approached. "Off to primp?"

"Unfortunately," Adeline muttered. "You all good here?"

"Absolutely," the petite brunette said with a confident nod. "I can't get over how amazing everything looks. I'd have never thought emerald green for the accents and bright orange for the flowers, but the contrast is amazing. Also, how the heck did you get Jean-Martin to cater? I've heard he never agrees to private events, even for Jada."

"I promised the mayor would attend the soft opening of his new Tribeca bistro, and take a photo."

"The mayor was cool with that?" Luciana said, distractedly adjusting one of the flower arrangements on a rented cocktail table. "I thought he doesn't usually trade in favors."

"He doesn't *exactly* know yet," Adeline said. "I figured I'd let him be dazzled by the food tonight, then spring it on him."

"Ask for forgiveness instead of permission," Luciana said, nodding approvingly. "Ballsy."

"Or career suicide. We'll find out. Okay, I have to go change. I'll have my phone the whole time. I'm still thinking I could use a headset. I can wear my hair down, nobody would have to know . . ."

"Absolutely not," Luciana said. "The party's not that big. I'll find you if there's anything I can't handle. Plus, you deserve to have fun. You've been working your butt off on this event."

"I've just been doing my job."

"I know. Doesn't mean you can't enjoy the fact that the Man of the Year personally invited you to his party."

"It wasn't like that."

Although maybe it was like that. She didn't exactly know how to define whatever was simmering between her and the mayor.

"Is he still not here yet?" Luciana asked, looking around.

"Trust me, we lucked out with him having that all-day fund-raiser in Long Island," Adeline said, picking up her garment bag and tote from the corner of the room.

But he would be back any minute, and Adeline was annoyed to realize she had butterflies. The type where you couldn't quite figure out if they were from nerves or anticipation.

She also couldn't figure out if the anticipation was because she was eager to see what he'd think of the surprise she had planned for the party, or simply because it had been a few days since she'd seen him, and . . .

She missed him?

No, that couldn't be right. She barely knew the guy.

And yet . . . he took up way too many of her thoughts. Even more annoyingly, it had been nearly impossible to focus on her date last week because she'd kept picturing another man, realizing that fancy Italian and a jazz club with Jane's coworker hadn't come close to greasy pizza and listening to Michael Bublé in the mayor's living room.

With a last few instructions for Luciana, Adeline hurried back toward the mayor's office, hoping she could catch Darlene before she headed out.

No such luck. Instead, it was one of the interns, a fresh-faced blonde named Megan whom she'd gotten to know over the past week as she'd dropped off stuff for the party.

"She left an hour ago," Megan said. "But she told me you'd be coming by, possibly looking for a place to change?"

"Yes," Adeline said, relieved. "I could make do with the public restroom, but . . ."

"Yuck, no," Megan said, opening a drawer and rummaging around for keys. "It's clean and all, but you can't get black-tie ready in there.

Besides"—she held up the key ring and gave it a little wiggle before lowering her voice—"I've always wanted to see the mayor's living quarters."

"His—What? No. I can't change there. Honestly, a closet would be fine."

"Darlene specifically said that I was to show you upstairs."

Adeline hesitated, mainly because the girl looked terrified that she'd get in trouble if Adeline balked at the instructions she'd been given. "Fine," Adeline said reluctantly. "I'm sure the mayor has a guest room I can use." She already knew that he did, but she wasn't about to advertise that she'd already been in the mayor's personal space.

Adeline let Megan lead, noting the way the handful of security milling about didn't look surprised to see them heading toward the mayor's private quarters. Darlene had clearly briefed them to expect Adeline.

The question was, had the mayor briefed Darlene? Or was she acting of her own accord, in female solidarity, just trusting that Robert wouldn't mind?

"I really appreciate this," Adeline said, unapologetically fishing for information from the intern. "Tell Darlene thanks for me."

"Sure," Megan said with a smile as she unlocked the door at the top of the stairs. "But actually, it's Kenny you should thank. Actually . . . Kenny's wife. She apparently learned you'd be at the party as a guest and said that you'd need a place to change."

"Oh," Adeline said, feeling deflated at the information. "That was thoughtful of her. And Kenny."

"Yup! You need anything before I head out?" Megan stuck her head through the door, looking around curiously. "They didn't tell me where specifically you should change, but I'm sure there's a powder room."

"I'll find it. And just to make sure the mayor's not in for an unpleasant surprise . . ."

"Kenny said he'd let him know that you'd be up here. Just . . . you know. Don't be, like, naked in his living room." Megan winked. "Have fun tonight!" she chirped, before closing the door, leaving Adeline alone. At least she was pretty sure she was alone.

"Hello?" she called. "Mr. Mayor?" She took a few steps toward what he'd gestured to as the master bedroom during the tour. "Mr. Mayor?" Adeline slowly pushed open the door and called again.

Nothing.

Confident she was alone, she started toward the powder room, then, remembering how small it was, bit her lip and eyed one of the other open doors. She found a moderately sized guest room with an attached bathroom and a full-length mirror, much better suited for party prep. It had probably been used for past mayors' family members, but since this mayor was single and childless, it probably served as a rarely, if ever, used guest room.

Adeline hesitated only a moment longer before stepping into the room and closing the door. With any luck, she'd be changed and freshened up before he even knew she was here.

She groaned as she got the first close-up of herself. It was worse than she'd thought. Her usually tidy bun had turned into a flyaway mess, and she may as well have not even bothered with makeup that morning, because it had long since vanished.

Adeline pulled her hair straightener and makeup bag out of the tote. A fancy updo was out of the question, but she could at least get rid of the worst of the frizz.

Thirty minutes later, she had a respectable smoky eye and light pink lipstick, and her hair was long and straight around her shoulders.

Wrinkling her nose, she pulled the necessary strapless bra out of her tote, and making sure the door was locked, she did a quick lingerie swap and unzipped the garment bag.

She had been planning to wear a conservative black sheath dress that was stylish but demanded no second looks. But when she'd opened her closet door, she'd found herself reaching for a different dress entirely. Still black, still conservative enough to be appropriate for the occasion, but with a bit more skin and personality than Adeline usually allowed herself.

The dress's hem hit somewhere between her knees and mid-thigh, and it had a subtle sweetheart neckline with a hint of cleavage. Not *Addie* cleavage—her early-twenties self had rarely chosen anything that wasn't one sneeze away from a nip-slip. This dress had classy cleavage, and even still, it was the first time in a while that the girls had felt any fresh air.

The real star of the show, however, was the back of the dress, where the straps crisscrossed in an X to center in on an enormous bow that gave a playful femininity to what would have been an otherwise forgettable dress.

In the safety of her apartment, she'd loved the dress—in fact, with it on, she'd felt the most like herself in years. But as she slipped on the black heeled sandals and looked at herself in the mirror now, she felt strangely vulnerable.

The makeup made her eyes look wide and girlish, the glossy lips made her look younger than usual, and the loose hairstyle instead of her typical bun made her look like . . .

Addie.

Her stomach dropped out as she realized the dark hair was the only thing that kept her from looking exactly like Addie Brennan.

The thought should have terrified her, and it did. She in no way wanted to be associated with that part of her life. But she was also shocked by the thrill of familiarity. She looked and felt like her old self.

Here was hoping *she'd* be the only one to note the similarities.

Luckily, she had access to the guest list and had been through it enough to know that while she recognized several names, most were limited to city politics. None were from her father's inner circle. She'd also paid extra attention to any media names on the list and had been relieved to see that the mayor had opted for newer faces on the press scene. Unless they had a party crasher, there'd be no sign of the paps who'd once followed her every move and every misstep, of which there had been many.

Going tonight was still risky, but she was going for it. Perhaps she was going for it *because* it was risky, because for all the potential pitfalls, she felt decidedly excited.

Adeline had started putting her makeup away and stuffing her clothes into her bag when she thought she heard a popping noise from the other side of the door.

Zipping up the bag, she opened the door a crack and blinked in surprise at the sight of the mayor of New York City holding two glasses of champagne, and not looking the least bit surprised to see her.

"Mr. Mayor?"

"Any chance of you calling me Robert?" he asked with a smile.

She stepped all the way into the living room, and his smile froze as his gaze drifted over her in frank masculine appreciation. To his credit, he dragged his eyes back to her face almost immediately, but it didn't diminish the warm, tingling feeling she felt everywhere.

"I didn't hear you come in," she said, feeling awkward as she set her bags by the door. "I'm so sorry if this is weird. I said I could change downstairs, but—"

He approached with the sparkling wine and handed her a flute. "Kenny told me. I don't mind."

"So, do you have all your employees change in your guest room?"

"You're not my employee." He clinked his glass to hers.

"You're paying me for a service."

He lifted his eyebrows. "Tawdry phrasing, Ms. Blake."

"Only if you interpret it like a perv, Mr. Mayor."

He choked a little on his champagne. "See, this is why I need you around. I don't think anyone's ever called me a perv in my life."

She shrugged and took a sip of the champagne. She tilted her head when she realized what he was wearing. "You're already dressed? Do you come out of the box in a tux or something?"

"I've been home for a couple minutes. Bow ties are tricky, but not quite as elaborate as . . ." He waved his flute over her.

"Oh, I have a bow, too!" she said, impulsively turning around to show him her favorite part of the dress. "See?"

The mayor's response was just a beat too slow in coming, and sounded a little rough. "Yes, Adeline. I see."

She froze at the sound of her first name, realizing it was the first time that he'd used it. But when she turned around, keeping the motion slow and casual, to search his face and see if he realized it, it was unreadable.

"Ready to show me your handiwork?" he asked, nodding toward the door. "You can leave your stuff here."

"You haven't seen downstairs yet?"

He shook his head, and she felt a rush of pleasure that she'd get to see his face when he saw the party setup for the first time.

"Absolutely." She started to set her champagne down on a table, but he shook his head.

"Take it with you."

"But I can't—"

"My house, remember? At least for a couple more weeks."

Her heart twisted at the regret she heard in those words, but she still shook her head. "Your house, yes. But I'm still the event planner. Not your personal guest."

The mayor opened his mouth, and she knew he wanted to argue, but he nodded in acknowledgment. "Fine. But I'm taking mine."

"As you should," she said with a smile as he opened the front door for her.

"Okay, so it's not going to be quite ready yet," she explained, unable to keep the excitement out of her voice as they headed downstairs. "We still have—" Instinctively, she reached out to tilt his watch hand toward her, since she'd taken her own watch off when she'd gotten dressed. "An hour," she said, reading the time.

He glanced down at her, and she bit her lip, realizing that one did not simply manhandle the mayor of New York City's left hand.

"Sorry," she said, belatedly registering the heat of him, even through the French cuff of his white sleeve. She dropped his hand. "I get a little excited right before an event."

His gaze locked on hers. "Did you hear me complaining?"

Her breath caught as she realized they'd both stopped walking at the base of the stairs. It was a quiet no-man's-land of the mansion—not his offices, not the event space, but not quite his private quarters, either.

They were trapped in between private and public, trapped in between professional relationship and . . . friendship?

Not friendship. Not *just* friendship, anyway.

Friends didn't look at friends the way the mayor was looking at her. The way she suspected she was looking back at him.

He leaned in—or was it her imagination?—and Adeline realized that she wanted him. She wanted to taste the champagne on his lips, wanted to muss his bow tie, wanted to—

"Mr. Mayor?"

His head snapped up, and he glanced over the top of hers. "Yeah. Charlie, what's up?"

"I apologize, sir. I didn't mean to interrupt. We just were trying to locate you."

"Sorry about that." He didn't sound sorry at all.

As they walked into the main hallway, she lowered her voice. "Did you seriously give your bodyguards the slip?"

"It's weird, they don't seem to approve of me trapping pretty women in darkened hallways while carrying booze."

"Very odd," she said with a smile, both relieved and disappointed that the strange moment had passed. Then disappointment was replaced once more by those anxious, excited butterflies as she remembered he was about to see her hard work from the past few weeks.

She was always expectant when a client was about to see her work, hoping she'd exceeded expectations, but it felt extra important tonight. Especially since she'd taken a big risk at a formal black-tie event for a powerful elected official.

"Wow," he said, sounding genuinely pleased as they stepped into the hallway where guests would get their first impression.

She'd kept this part elegant and relatively classic, with flower arrangements large enough to be impressive, but not so massive as to be in the way of milling guests.

They entered the ballroom, which was more of the same, though she'd taken a *bit* more risk here. In addition to the orange flowers contrasting the dark green tablecloths, she'd also brought in hundreds of white balloons to cover the ceiling with alternating orange and emerald strings.

"Too much?" she asked, biting her lips. "I wanted to bring a touch of modern into the otherwise stuffy space." Her eyes went wide. "Not *stuffy*, I just meant . . ."

His hand touched her back lightly. "Ms. Blake. It's perfect."

Pleasure at the praise mingled with displeasure that she was back to Ms. Blake, even though she knew it was for the best.

"Well, hold that thought," she said, gesturing for him to follow her into one of the parlors off of the main room.

He stepped into the smaller room with her, and she held her breath, waiting, since the "surprise" was fairly self-explanatory. Or so she thought.

Perhaps not. Because he still hadn't said anything . . .

Shit. "It's not too late to make it go away," she said in a rush. "We have extra tables and flowers, so we can make it a spillover room for people to gather . . ."

He continued to stare at the tables, each with a different board game. Monopoly. Scrabble. Battleship. Chutes and Ladders. Candy Land.

"It's a game room," he said quietly.

"You said you wished the parties could be a little more fun," she said. "And I thought it would be a fun dichotomy to have old-fashioned board games at a black-tie event. These things are usually staid—no offense—and I thought if we could combine formal with something a little more carefree . . ."

He touched her wrist, much in the same way she'd touched his earlier when looking at his watch. Except it wasn't the same.

She'd touched him almost accidentally. His touch was warm. Deliberate. Lingering.

"It's perfect," he said quietly, meeting her eyes, his hand dropping lower, fingertips brushing teasingly over her palm before he stepped away. "Absolutely perfect."

The butterflies were back.

But they had nothing to do with the party.

A couple of hours later, Adeline did yet another idle lap around the famed Wedgwood blue reception salon. She relaxed a bit more with each lap, relieved to see that not only were the guests seeming to enjoy the party but she'd heard a couple declare it the mayor's "best yet."

"Champagne?"

Adeline smiled at the server wearing a white tux shirt and black vest, almost telling him that she was the woman who'd hired him, then decided . . . what the hell. She'd done a good job. Everything was running smoothly. Luciana had the back of the house under control. And Adeline wanted to celebrate.

She accepted an elegant flute from the silver tray, along with a dark green cocktail napkin with the Manhattan skyline discreetly monogrammed in the corner.

"It's better than you'd guess."

"Hmm?" Adeline turned toward the unfamiliar voice as the server moved on.

A man who looked to be in his early thirties smiled at her, lifting his half-full glass of champagne. "The bubbly. It's quite good. You can tell Davenport dips into family money instead of city funds for his parties."

Davenport. Not a formal *Mr. Mayor*, but not a personal *Robert*, either.

"You're in politics?" she guessed.

He gave a friendly grin. "What gave me away?" The man shifted his glass to his left hand and extended his right. "Eddie Graham. Adviser to Glenn Covey."

Ah. Glenn Covey was one of two men running to take over the mayor seat in November. The race between him and opponent Ned Olivo had been a fairly acrimonious one, with both sides irritated at Robert's disinclination to publicly support either candidate.

"How do you fit into all this?" Eddie asked, gesturing to the room.

"I work for the mayor."

"Oh?" He tilted his head. "I thought I knew all the players, but I don't think I've seen you around. I think I'd remember," he added, letting his eyes linger on the neckline of her dress just a moment too long.

Adeline gave him a pointedly cool look as she took a sip of her champagne, letting him know what she thought of his *straight out of a political drama rerun* line. Although she was almost grateful for his understated sleaziness. It was a good reminder that she wanted no part of this world. She'd stay long enough to appease the mayor's insistence that she get a good read on the guests' mood, and then—

"Ms. Blake."

She turned, smiling when she saw the friendly face of the mayor's chief of staff. "Mr. Lamb! Good to see you again."

"You're killing me. Kenny, please." He turned to Eddie, his smile widening, although she could have sworn his gaze cooled just slightly. "Eddie. It's been a while. How are you?"

"About how you'd expect this close to Election Day."

"Right." Kenny turned to Adeline. "He tell you he's after my job?"

Eddie gave a short laugh. "Gotta get my guy in office first. Would sure help if *your* guy would back him up."

"You know, I just heard that exact same sentiment from Phil Day. Unfortunately, the current mayor is not a puppet."

"Or maybe it's not you who pulls the strings."

Kenny's affable smile never wavered, but the subtle shift in his posture had Eddie swallowing nervously. Adeline realized that for all of Kenny's easygoing schoolteacher vibes, he was no pushover.

"If you'll excuse us," he said, dismissing Eddie in a bored voice. "The mayor's asked that Ms. Blake spare a few minutes of her time."

Adeline let Kenny lead her away with a brief touch to her back. "Who's Phil Day?" she asked in a low voice.

"The guy who'll be chief of staff if Olivo wins."

"Ah, so that guy's nemesis," she said, pointing her head back to Eddie.

"Exactly."

"I was surprised to see the mayor invited both of them."

"*And* their bosses." Kenny stopped to grab a stuffed mushroom off a tray.

"Isn't that sort of inviting fireworks this close to the election?" she asked, shaking her head when offered a mushroom.

He gave an indifferent shrug. "The mayor always aspires to take the politics out of politics at these things. He says we're all just people and should treat each other as such."

"A noble stance, though perhaps an easier one to take when you're the most powerful man in the room."

"Is that a trace of cynicism I'm hearing, Ms. Blake?"

Adeline spun around to find the mayor looking down at her with a slight smile. "Um—"

He held up a hand. "No, you were right. It's certainly easy to spout lofty ideals from the top of the food chain."

"True. Though your track record indicates you do your best to make them a reality," she admitted.

His smile warmed. "Kenny," he said, without looking away from her, "mark the time and date as the moment I won over Ms. Adeline Blake."

"Don't go getting excited," she retorted. "I just meant you seem to put your money where your mouth is compared to a lot of politicians."

A certain politician in particular came to mind.

He leaned down. "Does that mean I can count on your vote in the next election?" he asked in a mocking whisper.

His words were meant as teasing—and they would have been harmless had he been talking to Adeline Blake, event planner.

But he was also talking to Addie Brennan, daughter of Governor Brennan.

She'd known it was coming. The signs had been there, the rumors were rampant. But hearing it out loud felt a bit like a thousand pieces of glass clattering to the floor. Or maybe those were just the pieces of her heart, the undisputable confirmation of something she kept forgetting: Robert Davenport would soon be a candidate for governor. And she, as the daughter of his opponent, couldn't be anywhere near him. As a friend, event planner, or otherwise.

"Next election? So you are running for governor?" She forced herself to ask the question, figuring if she heard it point blank, it would be the impetus she needed to keep a professional distance.

She could have sworn she heard Kenny groan under his breath, but she didn't look away from the mayor.

His eyes met hers steadily, though there was the slightest flicker of something . . . Regret? Uncertainty? "Nothing's official," he replied, "but—"

She held up her hand. "I don't want the spin version, Mr. Mayor. Yes or no."

He swallowed, his Adam's apple distinct against his bow tie. "Yes."

She gave a stiff nod, knowing her reaction was odd—no event planner should care this much about his political career—but she was unable to manage even a fake smile as she mustered a polite response. "Congratulations. Best of luck, Mr. Mayor."

Her voice was flat and a little cold. She heard it, and he must have, too, because his eyes narrowed.

"Best of luck?" he repeated, lightly mocking. "I'm not some stranger you've just met. A couple of hours ago you were naked in my apartment."

"Don't say it like that," she hissed. "You know full well there's nothing sexual between us."

"No?" He moved closer, and Adeline stepped back too quickly, losing her footing on the stiletto heels. The mayor reached out, setting a hand to her back to steady her, and she gasped at the contact of his palm against her bare flesh.

She slowly slipped away, her smooth movements belying the pounding of her heart as she turned and made her way toward the side of the room.

"Ms. Blake. Wait. *Adeline.*" His fingers hooked around her upper arm and pulled her gently around. "Where are you going?"

"I need to check on the caterers."

"The caterers—What—"

She pulled her arm aside, a quick glance around the room verifying they were getting several curious looks.

"Please," she said softly. "I don't belong here."

"You seemed to be doing just fine earlier."

I was pretending. "You don't know me," she said, reaching for the door.

He shifted his weight slightly, not blocking her way, but forcing her attention back to him. "So let me," he said softly. "*Let* me get to know you."

For one gut-wrenching moment, she wanted to. She wanted to let her guard down with this man who'd proven to be as kind, honest, and caring as they came. If he were anyone else—literally, anyone else—she might consider it. But that was exactly the problem. Somehow she'd let herself forget who he was. He'd spun the perfect web of charm and friendship and goodness, and she'd come so close to getting stuck.

But he'd just reminded her who he really was—a title first and a man second—and he had more power than anyone to hurt her. She had to get out of the web *now* before she had no chance of escape.

"Please. Leave me alone," she said quietly. "I don't want . . . this." Adeline gestured between them and, with a quick shake of her head, turned to walk away, only to come up short as she nearly ran into another man.

"Pardon," the other man said, the expression on his face unapologetically speculative as he gave her a once-over, then looked between her and the mayor.

She'd been about to excuse herself and brush by the stranger, but she paused and gave him a second look, because he knew her but she was quite sure she'd never met him.

He extended a hand. "Martin Tillman. The mayor's campaign manager."

She almost laughed. If she needed another sign that she and the mayor were oil and water, it was right here in this man, whose literal job was to keep the mayor in the public eye and to systematically crush anyone or anything who might taint his public image.

"Good luck with the upcoming election," she said, her voice kinder, less cold this time. She was surprised to realize she meant it. It had taken all of five minutes of meeting the mayor to know he'd make a better leader than her father ever would.

"Yeah, thanks," Tillman muttered, giving her another of those speculative looks as she slid around him and headed out of the ballroom.

"Ad—Ms. Blake," the mayor called. His tone was firm, and she had no doubt that most of the time, people heeded his command.

Not this time.

She made her way back through the party and into a cab, without a backward glance.

Chapter Fourteen

Monday, October 26

"I don't get it. How have you known the woman nearly a month, and still not know what she's been doing the past few years? Even where she's been living?"

Robert didn't look up from the pamphlet he was leafing through as he answered his agitated campaign manager. "Because she's a professional. How many people do you know who go spilling their life stories to clients they've known less than a month?"

"Bullshit."

This time, Robert did look up. "Excuse me?"

Oblivious to the warning note in Robert's voice, Martin didn't stop pacing around his office. "I know what I saw that night of the party, and it didn't have shit to do with the damned appetizers."

"Easy," Kenny said from where he stood, leaning against the corner of Robert's office, his preferred spot for "spectating," as he called it.

"And where the hell were *you*?" Martin snapped at the chief of staff. "Isn't it your job to make sure he doesn't go off the rails and get seduced by the one woman on the planet guaranteed to cost him the governor's seat?"

"Martin," Robert said, keeping his voice deliberately calm, "there are plenty of campaign managers out there. I'd be happy to hire one if you can't get your head out of your ass."

Martin shrugged out of his suit jacket and tossed it onto the back of a chair before dragging his hands over his face, clearly trying to get himself under control. "I'm sorry," he said. "But, Robbie, if there's something going on between you and Addie Brennan, I need to know it now so I can get ahead of it."

Robert reined in his knee-jerk instinct to remind Martin that she had the right to be known as Adeline Blake now, as well as to keep from asserting that a potential relationship between him and Adeline was nothing to get ahead of.

"We're friends. Don't forget that we hired her as much for her career as we did her father," Robert pointed out instead. "She was there to plan a party, and that's what she did."

"And now that the party's over, now what?" Martin snapped, hands on his robust waist.

"You tell me," Robert snapped back. "This was your plan."

"Yeah, well, I thought you'd have gotten something by now. You haven't learned a single useful thing?"

Robert heard Kenny shift slightly behind him, no doubt wondering why Martin didn't know about Adeline's mother not dying in childbirth.

Or maybe Kenny did know. Maybe Kenny had known all along what Robert was just now beginning to suspect—that Martin Tillman wouldn't hesitate to use the information in a way that would hurt Adeline as much as it did her father.

Robert shrugged. "It's like I said. Most people don't spill their guts to their client. She's a professional."

Martin snorted. "Professional, my ass. Have you googled Addie Brennan? The third search result is titty pics."

Robert felt anger curl through him, his fist clenching under the desk, though he kept his voice carefully impassive. "Look, you had a plan, we took a stab at it and came up empty. There's got to be another way to win this thing than just discrediting Brennan."

"True," Martin said, reluctantly dropping the Adeline topic. "It's the city's worst-kept secret that you'll be announcing your candidacy the second the new mayor's sworn in, so we're getting a better sense of the pulse."

"And?"

"Well, Man of the Year both hurt and helped," Martin said, pulling out a chair and plopping down. "Among millennials you're more popular than ever, but we know they don't vote like Gen X and baby boomers."

"I've always polled well with them."

"As a young man early in his career, yes. But it's like I said—you're not a twentysomething marvel anymore. The same things that made you popular in your twenties are hurting you in your thirties."

"Meaning?"

"The single status is starting to hurt."

Robert shrugged. "What do you want me to say?"

"Not say. Do. Would it kill you to go on a goddamn date?"

Unless it's with Adeline Blake, maybe.

The thought was absurd. He couldn't date Adeline. Even if she said yes, and that was looking increasingly unlikely after the party, it was too risky. A relationship with Adeline would be a bit like walking through a minefield. Fine, as long as they avoided all things Addie Brennan.

One wrong step, and he wasn't the guy dating the elegant event planner. He was the guy dating his opponent's wild daughter.

A file slapped onto his desk, and with a questioning look at Martin, Robert picked it up.

Kenny looked over his shoulder and whistled. The woman in the photo was stunning. Her dark eyes were wide and intelligent, her lips full and sensual, the rest of her features classically beautiful but unique enough to be arresting.

Robert lifted the photo, unsurprised to see that the rest of the file was a dossier on the woman. He also knew what Tillman had in mind.

On paper, the woman was the ideal partner of a governor hopeful. Her New York roots would appeal to those born and raised here, and her double degrees in sociology and economics spoke of someone with varied interests and balanced perspectives. Her quick rise through the entrepreneurial network to become a marketing director of one of the most buzzed-about start-ups of the last decade was every bit as impressive as the testimonials, which painted a picture of a woman both sharp and kind, funny and generous. She'd even played golf in college, just as he had, and still listed it as one of her favorite hobbies, just as he did.

She was, in other words, exactly the sort of woman he should be pursuing. He could barely stomach the thought. All of his attention was focused on another woman, who wanted nothing to do with him.

Irritatingly, Martin had been right when he'd accused him of being seduced by Adeline. The fact that she had done so by accident was humiliating. The fact that she hadn't been seduced by him in turn was as frustrating as it was motivating.

He flipped back to the first page of the file, frowning as he sensed he was missing something.

Rosalie. It was an unusual name, and yet he was certain he'd heard it recently. He searched his memories, filtering through conversations over the past few weeks, trying to figure out where a Rosalie had popped up in conversation . . .

Robert went still as he realized where he'd heard that name. And from whom.

From Adeline.

Their first lunch together, she'd mentioned her friend Rosalie. Had even suggested setting them up.

"You can't be serious," he told Martin.

"What am I missing?" Kenny asked.

The campaign manager pointed at the folder. "That woman is one of Adeline Blake's closest friends. And they went to the same high school."

Kenny caught on immediately. "So this Rosalie knows Adeline Blake and Addie Brennan are one and the same."

"One of the few who does, from what I can tell," Martin said. "There's another friend, but she's got a longtime boyfriend."

"Why does that matter?" Robert asked, even though he already knew.

Martin gave him an impatient look.

"*That's* your plan?" Robert asked. "You want me to date her friend?"

"C'mon, it's fucking brilliant! You'll get a picture-perfect girlfriend, possibly even the next First Lady of New York—"

"You're getting *way* ahead of yourself," Robert interrupted. "And how do you envision this happening? I somehow accidentally bump into them and angle for an introduction?"

"You said yourself you and Addie Brennan were *friends*," Martin said, putting a slightly mocking emphasis on the word. "And what do friends do, if not set each other up with compatible mutual friends?"

Robert cracked his knuckles, barely realizing he was doing so. The thought of going out with Adeline's friend made him slightly queasy. The thought of asking Adeline to make that happen made him extremely queasy.

Unfortunately, the thought of losing the election to George Brennan because he was hung up on a woman was equally unappealing.

"I like her," Kenny said quietly.

He glanced over his shoulder. "Rosalie? You don't even know her."

Kenny shook his head. "Adeline. She's somehow hard to read and authentic, all at the same time."

Robert shrugged as though it didn't matter one way or the other, but he knew as soon as he heard the words that his chief of staff had nailed the description. Adeline was both complicated and simple, cunning and forthright, vulnerable and shatterproof.

"I like her," Kenny repeated, "but Martin's got a point."

Robert's stomach tightened in dread. Those weren't words the Martin-averse Kenny would utter easily. "About?"

"Everything," Martin muttered.

Kenny and Robert ignored him. "Dating your event planner might raise some eyebrows. But dating your opponent's hell-raising daughter could be a career killer."

"Who said anything about dating Adeline?" Robert said. "I'm not even close to dating her."

Kenny gave him a look. *Everyone in this room knows you want her.*

"Kenny's right," Martin said.

"Since when have you two ever seen eye to eye?" Robert snapped.

"Since you became Man of the Year, bringing your bachelor status into unflattering focus. Since you got a hard-on for the incumbent's daughter, yet haven't learned a single thing from her that we can actually use."

"I don't have a hard-on for anyone," Robert snapped.

"Prove it," Martin said. "If she's just a friend, if she's just your event planner, ask for her friend's number."

Robert wanted nothing more than to tell his campaign manager to fuck off, but something stopped him. The fact that Martin had helped him win two mayoral elections. The look on Adeline's face when he'd told her he'd be running for governor. Her dismissal when he'd practically begged for a chance.

Please. Leave me alone. I don't want . . . this.

Robert picked up his phone, and before he could rethink it—before he could think at all—he did what gave him the best chance of getting an edge in the election.

He texted Adeline Blake and asked for her friend's phone number.

"Happy now?" he asked Martin as he tossed his phone back on the desk, cracking his knuckles again.

"Yes," the campaign manager said. "And you will be, too, when you see taking my advice will lead us straight to the governor's mansion." Martin paused for a moment and cleared his throat. "Your father would be proud."

Robert gave a distracted nod, suspecting that Martin was only half-right. His father would have been thrilled to know that Robert had served well as mayor and was moving up to the governor's seat, which historically, was a stepping-stone to the White House.

Everything he'd wanted was within reach.

Except . . . happiness.

And Robert was getting the sinking feeling that he'd just put a nail in the coffin of his chance at being happy with Adeline Blake.

Chapter Fifteen

Saturday, October 31

Adeline did a double take when her friend's name appeared on the screen of her phone, not with the usual text notification but with the persistent buzz of an incoming call.

"What's wrong?" Adeline asked, picking up immediately.

"Why would something be wrong?" Jane asked.

"Because I literally can't remember the last time you called me instead of texted."

"It's an emergency. I mean, I'm trapped in the Jersey suburbs on Halloween. I told Dan I had to take an urgent work call. That's you."

"Ah." Adeline tore open a mini bag of peanut butter M&M'S with her teeth and plopped on the couch. "I thought you were looking forward to passing out candy at Dan's parents' house."

"I thought it was going to be a way to show his parents that I was the mothering, adorable type. Restrained and maternal enough to tell the little darlings at the door to take just one, but playful and fun enough to dress up."

"And?"

"Well, for starters, I'm the only one over the age of ten dressed up. His eleven-year-old brother is wearing argyle. Unironically. Also, his parents aren't even here; they went to some party. Also, children are monsters."

"What'd you dress up as?" Adeline asked, popping an orange M&M in her mouth. They'd always been her favorite. So feisty, so underrated.

"Sulu," Jane said, referring to her favorite *Star Trek* character.

"Naturally." Over the years, Adeline had seen a lot of her friend's Halloween costumes. Sulu had made many appearances.

"What about you?"

"Sexy nurse," Adeline said, glancing down at the minuscule white costume.

"Oh, from senior year! I love that one, mostly because your dad's reaction was so much better than any disaster film I've ever seen."

Adeline winced at the memory. "In his defense, I was seventeen."

"In his defense, nothing. He acted like an ass, but then, I guess he always acted like an ass."

"Truer words."

"Tell me you're doing something fun with that slutty costume," Jane demanded. "I refuse to let anything that short and low-cut go to waste, even if you did reject my guy's suitorship for your hand."

"*Suitorship* isn't a word, and I didn't reject him," Adeline explained for the tenth time since her mediocre date with Jane's colleague. "I had a nice time, just not quite nice enough to want to do it again."

"Fine. But that still doesn't mean you should be hibernating in your apartment. It's Halloween. On a Saturday. That would have been Addie's Christmas."

Adeline smiled. She always had loved Halloween. She *still* did, hence the spontaneous decision to haul the nurse costume out of her closet, half with the vain experiment of wanting to know if it still fit (barely), as well as justifying having candy for dinner if she leaned into the holiday at least a little.

But venture out into the city alone on one of the craziest nights of the year? She wasn't feeling it. Especially since Jane was trapped in the suburbs, and Rosalie was . . .

Adeline tipped the M&M'S bag back and dumped the remaining pieces into her mouth at the thought of her friend. She didn't know what Rosalie was doing, but she had a pretty good idea of who she was doing it with.

She'd given Robert Rosalie's phone number less than a week ago, and already they'd been out on three dates.

Three dates.

Since Monday.

Adeline had barely talked to Rosalie, and she definitely hadn't talked to Robert, but as far as the media was concerned, they were a hit.

She'd seen the paparazzi photos of them at dinner, and again at lunch just two days later. Simply put, Rosalie *looked* like the woman who should be sitting across the table from the Man of the Year. The mayor apparently thought so, too. He'd been grinning or outright laughing in every picture.

She crumpled up the M&M'S wrapper, just as the repeated peal of the doorbell sounded on Jane's end of the conversation. Her friend muttered a curse, followed by a *gotta go, talk later, don't be pathetic, love you, bye.*

Adeline pushed herself off the couch, debated a mini Snickers bar, and decided the occasion was better suited to a glass of wine. She poured herself a generous glass of cheap Chianti and was debating between *Hocus Pocus* and *Halloween* when the phone by her door buzzed.

"I'm popular tonight," she muttered, going to pick up the phone that connected to her doorman downstairs. "Hi, Jamie," she said, getting the weekend evening doorman.

"Good evening."

She looked at the phone in confusion. *Good evening* was a strangely formal greeting for someone she'd just seen twenty minutes earlier and had gotten into a heated debate with over the merits of Jolly Ranchers. (Her stance: waste of time. They took too long, preventing one from getting to other, better candy. But Jamie insisted the fact that they lasted so long prolonged the payoff. To which she'd said he didn't even know the meaning of payoff if he thought a lemon Jolly Rancher could ever beat chocolate, and so on. Needless to say, their rapport was not of the sort where he was usually this deferential.)

"Did 4A give the delivery guy the wrong apartment again?" she asked.

"No, ma'am."

Adeline's eyebrows went up. *Ma'am?* Something was definitely up.

Her building wasn't fancy. There were maybe twenty units, and while the three alternating doormen were all nice and respectful, they'd also eaten buffalo wings while streaming the Jets game on their phones behind the desk and offered her some. And *she'd* accepted. In other words, they'd moved beyond *ma'am* within a week of her move-in date a year earlier.

"You have a guest. May I send him up?"

Her eyebrows went higher. She hadn't had a male guest in the entire time she'd lived here, and Jamie knew it. "Who is it?"

Jamie cleared his throat. "He's actually *already* on his way up."

"*What?* Jamie, you know you can't just—"

Realization hit her. She could think of only one reason why Jamie would be acting all formal and nervous, like the freaking president and his bodyguards were staring down at him.

Not the president. But damn close.

The knock at her door and verification out her peephole confirmed her suspicion.

"We'll discuss this later," she whispered to Jamie.

She hung up the phone as quietly as possible, not wanting to give any audible confirmation that she was home. There was zero chance she was opening her apartment to Mayor Davenport wearing a teeny-tiny nurse's costume.

"I already know you're home, because you picked up the phone when your doorman called," Robert said patiently through the door. There was a long silence. "Unless you're not alone and someone else picked up your phone . . ."

She rolled her eyes. As if she were dumb enough to walk into that one.

"Yeah, okay, that was a pretty bad fishing expedition," he continued when she remained silent. "You should just go ahead and take your time debating the merits of letting me in. In the meantime, I'll just chat up any of your neighbors who walk by and see the mayor practically begging to get into your apartment. Boy, to think of the rumors *that* will spur . . ." He let out a slow whistle.

She rested her forehead against the wall. Damn it. The only thing worse than the mayor being in her apartment was other people *knowing* he was in her apartment. If she let him in now, it was hopefully just his bodyguards, Jamie, and herself who'd know about his visit. If Adeline lingered and nosy Mrs. Teel were to take her Maltipoo on her evening walk and see him . . .

Adeline's hand went to the deadbolt and unlocked it, but she spoke through the door before she opened it. "You can't laugh."

"At what? Am I about to learn—"

She opened the door, and whatever the mayor had been about to say froze, his tongue seemingly stuck to the top of his mouth as he stared at her.

"Ah . . ."

"I thought you were known for having poise under pressure," she muttered, before reaching out a hand and hauling him inside her apartment. After a quick glance into the hallway to make sure none of her neighbors' doors were open, she closed hers.

The mayor still hadn't spoken. Nor had he looked away from her.

She crossed her arms, then realizing what that did to the deep V of the costume's neckline, dropped them again. "Go ahead. Point, laugh, make judgments. Just be quick about it."

Finally, he managed to drag his eyes up to her face. "I apologize."

She frowned, because it was the last reaction she'd expected. "For what?"

"Gawking?"

Adeline smiled in spite of her embarrassment. "It's ridiculous. I know."

"What, ah—what are you supposed to be?"

"A nurse, obviously."

"Obviously," he said distractedly. "Actually, no. I had knee surgery a couple years ago, and I distinctly remember the nurses looking *not* like that."

"I know," she said, glancing down. "It's pretty insulting to nurses, actually. I guess what I should have said is that I'm dressed up like one of those girls who thinks Halloween is just an excuse to wear the shortest, skimpiest outfit on the planet. I bought it when I was seventeen, saw it in my closet today, and—You know what? I didn't expect anyone to see me like this. I don't know why I'm explaining myself."

She put the slightest emphasis on *I'm* to let him know that he should be the one explaining himself, but he didn't get the hint.

"Mr. Mayor." She snapped her fingers by her face. "Up here."

He let out a laugh and ran a hand through his hair. "Sorry. I just . . . Are you wearing anything under that? No. Don't answer that. What were you saying?"

"What are you doing here? Actually, how are you even here? I know for a fact I've never given you my home address."

"Perk of being the mayor?"

She narrowed her eyes. "A legal perk?"

"We'll call it a loophole." His gaze started to drift downward again, and he gave a quick shake of his head and looked away, his gaze landing on her wineglass on the coffee table. He picked it up and took a healthy sip without asking, then another, looking around at her apartment.

"Most of my money went into the business and my office," she said, seeing the apartment through his eyes. The building was recently renovated, but it was an older style with small windows. Adding in the factor of her living on a low floor, there wasn't a ton of natural light, so she'd compensated by decorating mostly in whites and light neutrals to brighten the space as best she could. She actually found the simplicity of the decor soothing, but she supposed it also looked fairly plain.

"I like it," he said. "It feels like a home."

"Does Gracie Mansion not?"

"It's a home, just not *my* home. It's where I live, but I'm aware every day that plenty have lived there before me, and plenty will live there after me."

"The same would be true of the governor's mansion," she said, pouring a second glass of wine, since he had yet to relinquish hers.

He said nothing for a long moment. "It bothered you. The night of the party. To hear that I was running for governor."

Oh, you know, a little. Hearing it confirmed that you'd be going head-to-head against my father. Knowing that if you win the election, you'll be living in the same house where I spent some horrific teenage years.

Another thought hit her, this one even more painful than the first two . . .

Would the mayor raise his own children in the governor's mansion someday?

His and Rosalie's children?

The thought left a bitter taste in her mouth that she tried to wash away with a sip of wine, even as she decided to discuss the elephant in the room. "Did you come over to discuss Rosalie?"

He frowned. "Why would I do that?"

"Well," she said, pointing at him with her wineglass, "you're wearing jeans and a sweater instead of a suit, it's a Saturday, it's Halloween, you're the mayor, and I know you've gone on three dates with my best friend. I can't think of another reason you'd be here if not to discuss her."

He held her gaze. "Really. You can think of *no* other reason?"

That he held her gaze as he said it made her pulse leap even more than if he'd scanned her skimpy outfit.

He crossed his arms. "I just realized, I never asked. How did the date go?"

"What date?"

He gave a smug half smile at her response. "The one with your friend's coworker."

"Oh. Right. It was good. Great, actually," she exaggerated, because his satisfied smile at her initial response annoyed her.

"*Great*, huh? So you'll be seeing him again?"

"I'm thinking about it," she said primly, taking a sip of wine.

"What was his name?"

Adeline's mind went blank, and she frantically scrambled to remember the name of a man whose face she'd entirely forgotten. "Michael," she said, her relief at remembering it diluted by his smirk at her delay.

"And what's the verdict on jazz?" They both knew he wasn't asking about jazz, but about the man who'd taken her to the jazz club.

"Let's just say we didn't hit it off nearly as well as you and Rosalie." Her retort came more biting than she'd intended, leaving a thick layer of tension in the air.

They faced each other in the living room, the standoff strangely loaded given that she still wasn't sure why he was here uninvited, and yet strangely not unwanted.

"You're the one who gave me her phone number," he said, finally breaking the silence.

"Because you asked. You're welcome, by the way."

"I said thank you," he said quietly. "What did you expect? Was I supposed to send a lavish bouquet in gratitude for setting me up with your friend?"

She dug her fingers through her hair. "No. I don't know. But if you're planning to stay in my apartment, brooding and drinking my wine, I'm at least going to go put on a sweatshirt."

Like most Manhattan apartments, her living room was exceedingly small, the furniture taking up most of the space, and she had to brush by him to go back to the bedroom. Out of the corner of her eyes, she saw his fist clench as she walked by, as though resisting the urge to grab her arm to stop her. Even without the physical touch, the air crackled between them as she passed.

Distractedly, she pulled on an oversized gray sweatshirt. She contemplated changing into sweatpants as well, but she was behind on laundry and, she reminded herself, this was her apartment. If anyone should feel uncomfortable by her short skirt, it was the uninvited guest.

He was still in her living room when she reentered, though he'd moved to the window, staring out.

"Pretty view, right?" she said, knowing fully well he was looking directly into the darkened windows of an abandoned building that neighbored hers.

He turned around, his eyes dropping down to her sweatshirt as she pulled the too-long sleeves up to her elbows. "New Mexico?"

Adeline froze in the process of picking up her wineglass, then forced herself to finish the motion, casually taking a sip. "I picked it up from a souvenir shop in Santa Fe after the white shirt I was wearing lost a fight with chicken parmesan."

"I've never been."

She shrugged. "I lived there for a couple years."

"Santa Fe?"

"About forty-five minutes north in a little town you've never heard of."

"Manhattan must have seemed quite a change."

"Quite."

"Which do you prefer? Quiet desert, or bustling city?"

She was about to tell him it was none of his business, but she was a little surprised to find she wanted to tell him. So few people knew about her double life, so to speak, and the ones who did always seemed to tiptoe around the subject as though assuming she didn't want to talk about it. Which wasn't true. She'd cherished her time in New Mexico, just like she knew she'd made the right decision in leaving when she had. It wasn't a part of her life she wanted to bury, just keep secret from the wrong people.

And while Mayor Davenport should be near the very top of the list of wrong people, somehow he . . . wasn't.

"I like both," she answered. "Someday, after I get Jet Set to the point where I'm comfortable letting a team run it for long stretches at a time, I'd love to have a home in both places."

"Do you have family there?" he asked curiously.

Sadness had her glancing down at the ground instead of at him. "Not anymore."

He said nothing for a moment, then stepped forward to the candy bowl on her coffee table, pointing down at it. "Which is your favorite?"

She looked up, feeling both raw and frustrated. "Why are you here, Mr. Mayor? I know it's not to talk about New Mexico, or ask me my favorite kind of candy. Is it something to do with Rosalie—"

"Goddammit, will you stop bringing her up?" he asked, tossing a Kit Kat back into the bowl with so much force it bounced out again.

"You're the one who asked for her phone number!" she shouted back. "And now I feel like you're mad at me for doing exactly what you asked."

"I'm not mad," he said, throwing his hands up. "I'm just . . . What the hell, Adeline?"

"What do you mean?"

"What happened to us?"

"There is no *us*. I was your event planner. I did my job. Unless you have another event you want my company to consider, then—"

"I don't want your company," he said, taking a step toward her. "Don't get me wrong, I couldn't be more pleased with the way the party went, but that's not . . . it's not why I'm here. And don't start talking about your friend again, because she's not the reason I'm here, either."

"She should be," Adeline whispered. "You're perfect together."

"Are we?"

She swallowed. "She's pretty. Polished. Funny. Smart."

"And you aren't?"

"That's irrelevant."

His eyes narrowed. "All right. Allow me to ask something *relevant*. Does it bother you, even a little bit, to think of me with her?"

He reached out and pulled the wineglass from her hand, setting it on the table without breaking eye contact. He'd moved slowly, giving Adeline every opportunity to move away if she wanted to, but she stayed rooted to the spot, feeling the wall she'd erected to keep him out begin to crumble at his proximity.

"It doesn't matter," she whispered, her eyes locked on the center of his chest, because she didn't dare meet his eyes when he was this close. "You like her. That's what counts."

"You want to know why I'm mad?" he asked in a low voice. "It's because up until you gave me her phone number, I could believe that you felt what I was feeling. That you thought of me as often as I thought of you. That you enjoyed my company as much as I enjoyed yours."

I did. I do.

He lifted his hand to her face and lightly dragged the tip of his finger from the base of her ear along her jawline until it rested under her chin. "You see, when a woman sets a man up with her friend, he has no choice but to think her indifferent to him. To assume that it doesn't bother her in the least to think of him dating her friend, kissing her friend, making love to her friend." He stepped closer until there were mere inches separating them. "Rosalie is all the things you said. There's just one problem."

"What's that?" she whispered.

"She's not you."

His head bent down to her, and Adeline mustered every ounce of restraint to pull back slightly. "Don't. Please."

He swallowed, and she could tell from the way his eyes shuttered that her rejection had hurt him, but she wouldn't be that woman.

"You're dating my friend," she said.

"We've been on dates," he amended quickly. "Not *dating*. Very different things. I haven't kissed her. I haven't even held her hand. Hell, Adeline, aside from helping her with her jacket, I haven't touched Rosalie. I don't want to touch her. Not like I want to touch you."

She caught her breath, feeling yet another crack in the wall she was so frantically trying to keep between them.

"Rosalie's great. Really. But I won't be seeing her again."

"You won't?"

He shook his head. "It wouldn't be right. Not when I can't stop thinking about all the things I want to do with her friend. But what I need to know . . ." He took a deep breath, watching her face for her reaction. "I need to know if you want me back. Say no, and I'll back off. You won't see me again."

Adeline lifted a palm and set it to the center of his chest, her gaze locked for a long moment on her own fingers as she gathered her courage. Then she lifted her eyes to his. "And if I say yes?"

Robert's eyes turned immediately gold, and she saw a flash of cocky grin. Then he slid a hand around the back of her head and closed the distance between them as his mouth took hers.

All of the lies she'd been telling herself for weeks crashed down around her feet with each gentle, persuasive pull of his lips against hers.

She wanted him. She wanted Robert.

Adeline felt the last traces of her resistance crumble. She was stuck in his web. *Willingly.*

Her mouth opened to his, hesitantly, then more boldly, her body awakening to desires she'd thought long dead, but perhaps they had just been lying in wait.

For *him.*

He pulled back, a line appearing between his eyebrows as his gaze searched hers. "Adeline—"

She closed the distance between them, bringing their lips together once more, her fingers tangling in his hair to pull him closer.

He let out a slight groan at her response and wrapped an arm around her waist, yanking her body flush against his as his tongue parried with hers in a delicious promise. His hand slid down over her hip until he found the bare skin of her upper thighs, fingers leaving little licks of fire as they dragged over her skin. A moan escaped her lips as his hand slipped beneath the short skirt of her costume, pulling her even closer.

Somewhere in the back of her brain, she knew this was a bad idea for more reasons than she could possibly name. Or rather Adeline could name them; Addie didn't want to. For the first time in a long time, Addie won out.

He shifted her slightly, the back of her calves hitting the couch, their lips never leaving each other's as they collapsed onto the sofa in a tangle of limbs.

"*Yes,*" he said against her throat as her hands grew bolder, sliding beneath his sweater to the hot male skin beneath.

Her fingers explored the planes of his abs, sliding over the muscles of his back that proved he made time for the gym somewhere in his busy schedule. "This is crazy," Adeline moaned against his mouth.

"The only crazy thing is this sweatshirt." He hauled her into a sitting position just long enough to yank the bulky fabric over her head.

Her costume had shifted, courtesy of their frantic groping, the already low-cut V of her neckline now twisted so that it was barely containing her breasts, the lace of her black bra clearly visible.

Robert let out a quiet oath as he looked at her. The back of his knuckles brushed over the swells of her breasts, his gaze flicking to hers at the exact moment he let his fingertips slip beneath the lace.

Adeline let out a gasp as she arched up, but he continued to tease, his fingers nearly, but not quite, touching where she needed.

"Please."

"Please what?" he asked with a wicked smile.

She bit her lip and remained stubbornly silent.

Slowly he tugged the lace of her bra aside, intentionally letting the fabric graze her nipple but denying her his fingers. "Please what?" he asked again, his voice husky as his finger moved in ever tightening circles around the center of her breast.

Her eyes closed. "Please touch me."

"Please touch me . . . who?" His head lowered until his face was inches from the tip of her breast, his breath hot and torturous against her skin. "Say my name, Adeline."

Stubbornness mingled with need. "Mayor Davenport."

He let out a surprised laugh. "Good enough. For now."

Adeline cried out as his tongue lashed over her, her hands pulling his head toward her as his lips wrapped around her nipple.

He seemed to be inside her head, knowing when to tease, when to love, when to nip oh-so-lightly with his teeth. His fingers tugged aside the bra at her other breast, and he repeated the process all over again, until she was wiggling beneath him, gasping with need.

Desperately, she reached for Adeline's sanity beneath Addie's need, letting herself register what she must look like, a ridiculous nurse costume hiked up around her waist, the fully clothed mayor of New York City bent over her, making her crazy with want. "Wait," she said, her fingers tugging in his hair, lifting his head. "We can't do this."

He froze immediately, though the tension in his body told her the effort wasn't easy. "No?"

His eyes were both hungry and patient, letting her know what he wanted, while simultaneously promising that she was in control of the situation. It was the promise that scared her the most, because it confirmed what she'd suspected from the very beginning: that if she wasn't careful, she could fall stupidly, completely for a man who could never be hers, not when he learned who she really was.

Robert might want the woman in the tiny nurse costume, but eventually, he'd need the woman in the blazer—one who wore blazers for real, not as a disguise. And she cared about him enough to want that for him.

Adeline set a hand to his cheek, her palm savoring the soft scrape of his stubble. "I can't sleep with a client," she whispered. It wasn't the whole truth, but it *was* a truth. She was proud of what she'd accomplished with Jet Set, and this was not how CEOs conducted business.

His eyes slammed shut and his head dropped forward just for a second, letting out a slow, deliberate exhale. When his head lifted again, his eyes were more controlled. "I hate how much I understand and respect that."

Adeline felt simultaneous relief and panic—relief that he understood and panic as her heart registered men like him were as rare as they were wonderful.

He slowly climbed off her, retrieving her sweatshirt and handing it back to her with a playful smile of regret. "I will never look at a nurse in the same way again."

Adeline let out an embarrassed laugh as she pulled the sweatshirt back over her head and tugged down the hem of her twisted skirt, grateful to have something to do to prevent her from having to meet his eyes.

He cleared his throat as she continued to fidget with her clothes longer than necessary. "Adeline, about Rosalie . . ."

Her stomach knotted. "I don't want to talk about her. Not until I've had a chance to talk *to* her."

"You're going to tell her? About this?"

The knot in her stomach pulled tighter. "I'm not going to be the other woman."

"The—What?" His eyes flashed in anger. "Is that seriously what you think of me? That I'd date one woman publicly, and keep the other as a secret? I already told you I wasn't going to see her again."

"I know," she said tiredly. "It's just . . . you're a . . ."

"What?" he asked, when she broke off. "I'm a what?"

She blew out a breath. "Politicians aren't exactly known for their exemplary personal lives. Mistresses have been fairly de rigueur throughout history."

"Jesus." He dragged his hands over his face. "This was a fucking mistake."

She flinched. "Mr. Mayor . . ."

"See, that's the problem," he snapped. "You've got it in your head that all politicians are shit, and that's all you see me as, isn't it? An elected official, a figurehead."

No, actually the problem is that I keep forgetting it.

"You *are* an elected official," she said, needing to say it out loud to remind herself. "You're the mayor. A governor hopeful. A for-life politician, who'll never *not* be in the spotlight."

He sucked in a breath, then released it slowly. "I see. And I'm not worth the burdens that come with that?"

Adeline's chest ached at the look on his face, and she tried to explain. "We're so different."

He reached out and plunged his hands through her hair, tilting her face up to his, his eyes burning into hers. "That's just the thing, Adeline. I don't think we're all that different. I'm not a machine, and I'm not a puppet. I'm a man. I breathe, I think, and damn it, I *feel*."

Her heart seemed to stop beating in her chest, her thoughts, emotions, and memories all jumbled up into one unsolvable ball of confusion.

"I'm a man," he repeated, his thumb dragging over her lip, before he took a step back and released her. "Figure out what you want to do about that."

He walked out of her apartment without another word.

Chapter Sixteen

Sunday, November 1

The next morning, Adeline's under-eye concealer had some serious heavy lifting to do. She'd tossed and turned after the mayor had left her apartment, and she'd dozed off sometime around dawn, just in time for her alarm to go off to start what promised to be a difficult day.

Rosalie had always had a weakness for doughnuts, so Adeline was first in line when one of the city's most famous doughnut shops opened at six. Unsure whether her friend's tastes had evolved since high school, Adeline got plenty of Rosalie's old standby maple bars, along with an assortment of more exotic specialty flavors, including a mint chocolate one that she was hoping she might get to sample if Rosalie didn't throw her out first thing.

Armed with a dozen doughnuts, Adeline stopped into Starbucks near the Airbnb where Rosalie was staying. Her friend was between two leases and had opted for a temporary residence rather than settling for someplace she didn't love.

Expecting the usual Sunday rush, Adeline had placed a mobile order for two pumpkin spice lattes, an extra shot of espresso in her own. Somehow, she managed to get both cups and the box of doughnuts to Rosalie's front door without any spills. Not bad for someone who was painfully short on sleep.

She knew her friend would be awake because Rosalie had invited Adeline to a seven o'clock yoga class this morning. It gave them only a couple of minutes to talk before Rosalie would have to leave, but a couple of minutes was all it would take for Adeline to say what she needed to.

A man and his pug opened the front door to Rosalie's walk-up just as Adeline was trying to figure out how to ring the call button without spilling the coffee. She slipped inside and used the toe of her tennis shoe to gently knock on Rosalie's first floor door.

Her friend opened immediately, already dressed for yoga in sleek black pants, a hot pink workout top, her long black hair in a high ponytail.

"Hey! Come on in," Rosalie said with a warm smile. "You change your mind about yoga?"

"Definitely not," Adeline said, stepping inside. "I just brought pre-workout nourishment."

"Ah, yes, I'm sure this is exactly what all personal trainers would advocate," Rosalie said, opening the box of doughnuts Adeline set on the kitchen table. "Is that a marshmallow?"

"S'mores doughnut," Adeline explained, handing her friend a coffee.

"Not that I don't always welcome a sugar rush, but what's the occasion?" Rosalie asked, debating all the options before reaching for a maple bar.

Never one to beat around the bush, Adeline took a deep breath. "I have something to tell you."

"Shoot," Rosalie said, licking maple off her thumb.

Adeline looked her friend dead in the eye. "I kissed the mayor."

The brief pause in her chewing was the only sign that Rosalie had even heard her. She took another big bite of the doughnut, washing it down with a sip of the latte.

"Hello?" Adeline said, a little impatient to receive judgment so she could begin atoning.

"Was it hot?" Rosalie asked, waggling her eyebrows.

"*What?* I kissed your boyfriend, and that's your reaction?"

Her friend snorted and dropped into one of the kitchen chairs. "He's not my boyfriend. Not even close."

Adeline slowly sat in the other chair. "You've been on three dates."

"I've shared three meals with the man, with his bodyguards a few feet away, and about a hundred pairs of eyes on us. Those aren't dates."

"But you've been out with him three times in one week."

"Sure. I guess *technically* it's been three outings. I think we both kept agreeing to meet up *again*, hoping it would build some momentum and turn into something, but . . . nope. No spark. He thinks so, too, otherwise he wouldn't have kissed you. He doesn't strike me as the player type."

"But—" Adeline blinked, trying to sort out her thoughts. "You're supposed to be mad."

Rosalie smiled. "Well, I am a little mad that you set me up on a date with the guy you liked."

"I don't like him," Adeline said automatically.

"So, what, your lips accidentally fell on his? Or was it the other way around?"

Adeline grunted and took a sip of her coffee.

"So it *was* hot," Rosalie said smugly. "I knew it."

"It was a onetime mistake," Adeline said.

"But obviously there's chemistry . . ."

"Chemistry doesn't matter," Adeline said a touch sharply. "He doesn't know me. He has no idea that I'm really Addie Brennan, that he's about to run against my father, that he literally couldn't pick someone more unsuitable to be his arm candy."

"You could tell him."

Adeline scoffed. "Why would I do that?"

"Because protest all you want, but you *do* like him," Rosalie said softly. "The fact that you've avoided my texts all week after setting me up with him made me wonder. The fact that you've brought me grovel doughnuts after making out with him sort of proves it. And he likes you. His mind seemed a million miles away when I was with him, and I'd bet anything it was on you."

"He likes *Adeline*. He doesn't know—"

"You *are* Adeline!" Rosalie interrupted, leaning forward with impatience. "I know it's usually Jane who plays the tough love role, but I'm going to try my hand at it. This whole multiple personalities thing you've developed? It exists only in your head, and it's getting old. I can respect that you wanted to reinvent yourself. I even understand the name change in a world of social media bullshit where silly mistakes never quite go away. But you're not two people, so you don't get to pick and choose when you get to use Addie's demons as an excuse when Adeline feels vulnerable, nor do you get to use Adeline's career as a justification for ignoring who you really are."

Adeline pursed her lips. "Wow. That was . . . a lot."

Rosalie pushed the box toward her. "Doughnut?"

Adeline picked up the mint chocolate one and contemplated her friend's blunt assessment as she chewed. It wasn't exactly fun to have her issues so plainly spelled out before she'd finished her coffee, but she appreciated it all the same. Both that Rosalie cared enough to speak up and the clarity it provided.

Yes, she'd been hiding. Yes, she'd been using her past as an excuse when it suited her, and then just as easily using her present as a defense mechanism, all so that she could avoid that awful, burning feeling of not being good enough. And yes, she still had some work to do to figure out how to love herself because of her past, not in spite of it. And she would get there.

But.

It would never change the fact that there was one world where Addie Brennan's "sins" would never be forgiven, and that was Robert's world.

Her father may have been cruel when he'd pointed out that girls with topless photos on the web didn't belong in the governor's mansion, but he'd also been right. Her father knew it, Adeline herself knew it, and Robert knew it, even if he didn't know that Adeline was one such woman.

"You're not wrong about any of it," Adeline said, polishing off the doughnut as Rosalie picked up a second one, opting for a fancy lemon meringue option. "I need to learn to love myself, both the Addie and Adeline sides."

"I know," her friend said with a wide smile.

"But," Adeline added, "that doesn't change the fact that no amount of growth on my end, no amount of embracing my Addie side, will ever allow Robert Davenport to date Addie Brennan without serious consequences to his career."

"But—"

"No," Adeline said gently. "You know I'm right on that. This is the real world. The only reason my antics didn't ultimately cost my father his seat was because he was able to wash his hands of me, just as he did my mom. People can relate to and forgive a father cursed with a miscreant daughter. They won't relate to or forgive a man who chooses that kind of woman as his girlfriend."

Rosalie put her doughnut aside untouched. "This sucks."

"It does," Adeline said pragmatically. "And you're right, I do like him. Way more than I should. But it's because I do that I'd never ask him to choose between me—the *real* me—and his job."

Rosalie's eyes were sad. "You know, I've always been a little cynical about politicians. Not as much as you, but I always thought they did it for the power and ego trip more than anything else. But even I can see how much he lights up when he talks about his work."

Adeline nodded, relieved that her friend understood. Then she took a deep breath and brought up the other reason she'd come over with bribery doughnuts. "I have a favor to ask."

"Oh no."

"A little one," Adeline reassured her. "Well, actually, not so little. It's just . . . would you go on one more date with him? On Tuesday?"

Rosalie frowned. "Why Tuesday?"

"It's Election Night. They'll be voting in a new mayor."

"Election—*No*! Do you have any idea how many cameras will be on him? On me? On us?"

"Yes. And it's why I can't be there," Adeline said gently.

Rosalie was still shaking her head. "You just confessed that you like him. I'm not going to date the guy my friend's got a thing for."

"It doesn't have to be a real date," Adeline said softly. "He'd never admit it, but I think Tuesday's going to be hard for him. Being mayor wasn't just his job, it was his entire identity. That'll be essentially ending on Tuesday night, and I don't . . ." She took a breath. "I don't want him to be alone."

Rosalie stared at her a long moment. "Sweetie," she said gently. "You don't just *like* the mayor, do you? It's deeper than that."

Adeline didn't answer. Not to her friend, and definitely not to herself. Instead she gave Rosalie a beseeching look. "Please? Promise you'll be there for him?"

Her friend sighed as she picked up the doughnut once more. "Fine. But in exchange, I want you to tell me all about the kiss. If I'm not going to be hooking up with the Man of the Year, I want to hear every dirty detail from the woman who is."

Chapter Seventeen

Tuesday, November 3

There was a new mayor of New York City.

Ned Olivo—the man Robert privately believed was the better person for the job—had established a sizable early lead over Glenn Covey early in the day. The gap had only widened as the remainder of the votes came in, and Robert and Rosalie had been on their way to Olivo's campaign headquarters to offer their congratulations even before Covey had called to officially concede the race just before midnight.

Robert had been mentally preparing for this night for weeks now, and he'd thought he was ready. But shaking the hand of the mayor-elect and keeping a smile on his face had been a good deal harder than he'd expected.

Not that he wasn't happy for Olivo—he, better than anyone, knew the triumph of that moment. He wanted Olivo to have it, too.

And yet . . .

Robert idly rubbed a hand over his chest.

He felt raw. Empty. *Alone.*

Yes, he'd spent the past several hours in the company of people. Yes, Kenny had never left his side. And Rosalie, despite having surprised him by showing up in the first place, had been a lifesaver, absorbing a fair amount of pressure from the media and seemingly knowing exactly how to strike the right balance between saying the right thing and never taking the focus away from Ned and his wife, Pam.

The front-page news tomorrow would be about the new mayor, but Robert was reasonably certain that the more gossipy channels would have another lead story: the mayor's new girlfriend. Rumors about him and Rosalie had been swirling all week, and he knew her presence on Election Night would only clinch the assumption that they were official.

He didn't care. The media could report them married for all he cared, and he'd let it roll off his back because it wasn't true. He knew it, and just as importantly, Rosalie knew it. She'd quickly assuaged any concerns he had that she'd gotten the wrong idea by telling him at the start of the evening that she was there as a friend only.

He'd been grateful. For her. For Kenny's under-the-breath cracks designed to distract him. For the constant crowd of people who'd provided endless diversions all night.

And yet he'd never realized just how *alone* one could feel in a crowd of people. For all the good intentions, nobody had been able to ease the ache inside him. He wasn't even sure anyone was *aware* of the ache.

It was now three a.m., and he was dangerously close to cracking.

Robert bade a distracted good night to Charlie and the others on his security detail for the night, then entered the sanctity of the private living space of Gracie Mansion.

He shut the door and leaned against it, waiting for the usual sense of respite from the job that came with retreating to his private quarters. As he'd told Adeline, it had never precisely felt homey, and yet it *was* home—the only one he'd known for eight years.

Tonight, however, it offered little comfort. Tonight, it was yet another reminder that this stage of his life—what felt like his *whole* life—was at an end. In a couple of months, this would be someone else's home. Olivo would be sworn in in January, and Robert would be able to commit himself fully to the campaign trail.

If he won, it'd be off to the governor's mansion. Another job, another challenge, another home.

If he lost, he'd shift gears. Focus on *another* job, *another* challenge, *another* home . . .

And then what?

The thought nagged.

Looking ahead, all he could see was more elections. More terms. Followed by more elections, and then more terms . . .

Is that all there is?

Robert let out an irritated grunt at the haunting, meddlesome voice in the back of his mind. A voice that hadn't been there until recently, a voice that had only gotten louder after he'd met Adeline and let himself wonder what it would be like to do this whole thing *with* someone. To have a partner, not for show, but for real.

To have not a Rosalie. But an Adeline. *An Addie.*

He gave a harsh laugh as he poured himself a stiff drink from the sideboard. He didn't have Adeline. Or Addie. It didn't matter what he called her; the woman didn't even trust him enough to tell him her real name. And maybe she shouldn't. He hadn't exactly entered into their arrangement as an open book himself.

"You always laugh alone in the dark?"

Robert pivoted at the sound of the soft, familiar voice, his eyes searching through the shadows of his living room until he saw Adeline sitting on a tufted chair, legs crossed, posture relaxed, as though she belonged there.

"How the hell—"

"Kenny," she said, standing.

Robert continued to stare as she walked slowly toward him, registering he must be more tired than he'd originally realized, because he was having trouble comprehending her presence. "He called you?"

"I called him," Adeline said softly, stopping in front of him. She was wearing jeans and a baggy sweater that made her seem younger. Softer.

"Why?" he asked.

"I saw you on TV." Adeline slowly reached out and pulled the untouched bourbon from his hand and set it back on the sideboard.

"And? You realized your days of being able to claim personal acquaintance of the mayor of New York City were limited?" he asked, a little more snidely than intended, taking his raw emotions out on her because she was here.

"Not quite." She stepped closer, and before he could register her intention, slim arms wrapped around his waist, pulling his taller frame to hers.

He froze for a second, taking an embarrassingly long time to register the sweet, simple gesture for what it was. *A hug.*

One that packed a surprising wallop of comfort. Comfort he so desperately needed . . .

His arms closed around her, crushing her close and unapologetically absorbing every ounce of solace and consolation her arms offered.

She said nothing, only wrapped her arms tighter, her cheek pressed to his chest as though it belonged there. His chin rested on the top of her head as though *it* belonged *there.*

As though they belonged to each other.

He closed his eyes and felt the slight burn between his eyelids as he gave in to the emotions he'd been trying to keep at bay all night. Pride at what he'd accomplished over eight years. Grief that it was over. Relief that the man appointed as his successor seemed the decent sort. Uncertainty over what was to come. Sadness that he'd be facing it alone.

No, that wasn't right. Sadness that he'd be facing it without *her.*

When he opened his eyes, he felt decidedly steadier, as though her mere presence had absorbed his turmoil and smoothed out the roughest edges of it, allowing him to focus on what mattered most in this moment.

That she was here.

Robert ran a hand up her back. "Why'd you come?"

"You cracked your knuckles," she said, not lifting her face from his chest. "Just once, when Olivo was giving his speech and you were off to the side of the camera with Rosalie."

His hand paused for a moment, startled to realize that he'd been distracted enough to show that much emotion when there were cameras in the room. More surprised to know that Adeline had recognized the gesture for what it was.

He tensed a little at the mention of her friend, wondered if it had bothered her that Rosalie had been there, then remembered Rosalie had hinted that Adeline had all but insisted she attend. At the time, he'd assumed it was merely Adeline throwing Rosalie up as a barrier between them, but now he wondered if it had been more than that. If she hadn't sent Rosalie to be there for him in public, in a way she herself couldn't be.

Robert eased away so he could see her face, and the softness in her usually guarded gaze told him he was right. He lifted his hand, touching a thumb gently to her cheekbone, the softness of her skin nearly undoing him. "Thank you."

"You're welcome," she whispered.

The quiet darkness and the warmth of her embrace had offered comfort just moments earlier, but as their gazes locked and held—and held—the air around them seemed to change, becoming charged with the most primal of needs.

He slowly lowered his head, holding her gaze until the last possible moment when their lips touched, watching her eyes flutter closed, feeling his own close as he let touch and taste become his dominant senses.

Her mouth had been sweet with chocolate when he'd kissed her on Halloween, and it was even sweeter this time, simply because it was her. Sweet, and hot, with the little nip of spice that he'd come to associate with Adeline Blake, the promise that he could never, ever become bored with her.

On Saturday night, she'd been warring with herself, not wanting to want him. He'd been frustrated by it, even as he'd understood it all too well.

Tonight, neither of them fought it. She opened herself to him fully, and he took it. All the way.

Robert's hands slid beneath her sweater, smiling against her mouth as he registered that this ugly sweater was every bit as attractive to him as the sexy, ridiculous nurse outfit had been. His smile faded as he realized it wasn't the clothes that mattered, but the woman beneath them. A woman who was apparently irresistible to him. *Dangerous.*

She lifted her arms over her head, her blue eyes issuing a silent challenge. *Danger accepted.*

His hands found the hem of her sweater, lifting it up and over her head, careful not to tangle it in her long hair as he tossed it aside.

"I like your hair like this," he said, running his fingers through the length of it.

A little smile curved her lips. "I'm standing topless in front of you, and you care about my hair?"

I care about all if it.

Still, the man in him couldn't stop his gaze from drifting down to her chest, unable to stifle the groan at the sight of her without a top, her bra half-tangled around her torso.

The bra was red, lace, low-cut, and clearly intended to kill him.

"Jesus," he muttered, running a finger over the top swell of her breast, male satisfaction tightening his stomach when her breath caught. "Please say this is just for me."

"It's for *me*," she said. Then her gaze softened. "But tonight it might be a little bit for you, too."

Rewarding her for the admission, he bent his head to her breasts, wanting to tell her that her body was perfect—absolutely, sinfully perfect—but instead putting his mouth to better use, trailing kisses along the upper edge of the lace, teasing her as he had the other night, wanting to hear her beg again.

He didn't have to wait long. She whimpered in need, her hands coming to the back of his neck as he unhooked the delicate bra, tossing it alongside her sweater as he worshipped her beautiful breasts with his mouth.

She was built like every man's fantasy, he realized, as his hands explored her small waist, drifting farther to the swell of her hips. As he dropped to his knees, his fingers found the button of her jeans. He looked up to find her watching him, her expression uncertain for the first time since she'd come to him tonight.

"I'm glad you're here," he whispered, unfastening the button slowly, then pausing, waiting to see if she wanted him stop.

Her eyes closed, and her ragged breath egged him on.

Pressing a kiss just below her navel, he slowly slid her jeans down, groaning as he saw the V of her underwear matched the bra.

She helped him by kicking her shoes off and stepping out of the jeans, then froze when he slowly dragged the pad of his finger over the tiny scrap of lace. He nearly came undone at the realization that she was already wet.

Her eyes closed again as he teased her over the fabric, and he pulled his finger away, waiting for her eyes to open again, smiling at the frustrated scowl.

"Watch me," he commanded.

Her eyes narrowed but didn't close as he touched her again, this time more firmly. Back and forth, round and round, he circled her through the fabric of the panties, holding her gaze the entire time.

His breath was no steadier than hers when he finally dragged the lace down her legs. Her eyes closed again when he slid a finger into the seam of her sex, and he froze, waiting until she opened them once more.

"Watch me," he repeated, needing her eyes on him, needing her to know he was an absolute slave to her, worshipping everything she was.

He leaned forward, his tongue touching between her legs, and she cried out, her head falling back. Robert could have punished her for looking away by pulling away, but he'd be punishing himself as well, because he'd never wanted anything like he wanted to taste her, to bring her pleasure so intense she'd never forget him, or this moment.

He teased her with light strokes of his tongue, tormented her with his finger until she was gasping. Finally, he circled with his tongue in the exact spot that made her cry out. She came against his mouth with an unapologetic shout that his security detail could probably hear, but he didn't care, because she didn't care. For the first time, he sensed she was fully exposed to him, body and soul, and his chest tightened with the magnitude of the moment.

She was still breathing hard when he finally stood. He meant to carry her to the bed to let her catch her breath, but she lifted her hands to his shoulders with purpose.

Robert let her shove the suit jacket off his shoulders, let her yank at the tie, helped her make quick work of his cuff links and the buttons.

His shoes, socks, and pants were gone just as fast, and she reached eagerly for the bulge beneath his briefs, but he snagged her wrist and lifted her hand to his lips, giving her knuckles a quick kiss. "I've got about a month of wanting you built up. This could be over quickly, and I want to be inside you."

It was somewhere between a question and a plea, and she smiled in understanding, leaning forward to kiss his mouth as her free hand explored his chest. "Condom?"

Anticipation made him a little rough as he pulled her toward the bedroom, releasing her wrist only when she was on the bed, spread out to him like the most delicious gift he'd ever received.

He lowered on top of her, hands finding her face, lips claiming her mouth as he settled above her, nudging her opening. Even now, he couldn't satiate his need to see her, so he pulled back slightly, watching her eyes as he pushed forward.

Her eyes closed halfway, her chest rising and falling as her nails dug into his shoulders, urging him on. Only when he was all the way inside her did his eyes finally close, and he buried his face in her neck, registering that her body clamped around his was the most perfect sensation of his entire life.

He pulled all the way back, then thrust forward again, hard. She met his every move as he cupped her butt, thrusting harder, faster, until he took them both over the edge with unapologetic ownership of her body, even as he gave his own body over to her.

Neither moved for minutes after, until she finally gave his shoulder a half-hearted shove. "Heavy," she muttered.

With the last bit of his strength, he rolled off her, though he kept one arm around her to keep her close.

She didn't try to pull away, but after several moments of drowsy silence, she dragged a finger over his biceps. "I have to leave," she whispered. "I've got to be at work in just a couple hours, and we can't let anyone find me here."

It was a dose of reality he didn't want, but probably needed. Starting today, everyone's attention would shift away from the mayoral race of yesterday, and on to the governor's race of next year.

A governor's race in which he'd be running against a man whose daughter he'd just ravished, a daughter who'd nearly cost her father an election.

A woman who could very likely cost Robert the election.

Most terrifying of all, a woman who was making him want something *more* than the election.

Chapter Eighteen

Adeline had a plan. A good plan.

A *sexy* plan.

The plan had not accounted for rain. Or forgetting her umbrella.

"Hey, Darlene," she said to Robert's assistant, lifting her hand to her hair and wincing when she realized her bun was wet enough to be wrung out. "Is the mayor in?"

He'd told her this morning that he had the afternoon free, and she was hoping he hadn't booked any last-minute appointments.

"Ms. Blake! It's so good to see you. I didn't have a chance to tell you at the party how impressed I was. My husband usually hates those things, but he declared it the best party yet. I think it helped that he dominated anyone who dared to take him up on his Battleship challenge."

Adeline smiled. "I'm so glad he had a good time."

"Give me one sec, let me check the mayor's schedule . . . Looks like he's got a break between meetings. I'll see if he has a few minutes. Can I get you some tea first?"

Adeline looked knowingly down at her bedraggled appearance. "That bad, huh?"

Darlene smiled. "I heard there were going to be downpours today."

"Well, that makes one of us. I would have killed for an umbrella."

"At least you're wearing your trench coat!"

At least.

"Some tea would be great," she told Darlene. Not because she particularly wanted it, but because her plan necessitated the element of surprise, and Darlene announcing her arrival would mess that up.

"Give me just one second, and I'll fetch it myself," Darlene said, standing. "I swear, I thought things would be *less* busy around here after the election, but it's been chaos all week."

Adeline smiled in response, waiting until Darlene disappeared from sight before slipping around her desk and knocking on Robert's door.

"Yeah."

Taking a deep breath, she opened the door and stuck her head in, hoping to find him alone.

Robert was behind his desk, forehead propped on his hand as he read something on his tablet. He looked up, then did a double take. The slow smile that spread over his face was worth getting caught in the downpour.

"Hey. Come on in."

She stepped into the office as he came around his desk, his hands already reaching for her even as the door clicked shut.

"Darlene's bringing me tea," she said with a laugh that quickly turned to a moan as his lips found her neck beneath the collar of her jacket.

His teeth nipped gently against her throat as he reached behind her, locking the door with a flick of his thumb.

"Mr. Mayor—"

"Still with that? You've seen me naked. I think we're in a first-name kind of place," he said, his lips closing over hers.

She melted into the kiss, absorbing his warmth as she forgot about the rain, the tea, and the upcoming election. She forgot everything except how good it felt to be with him. To be in his arms, to feel his tongue slide against hers.

His fingers found the knot of her coat and tugged, but she grabbed his wrists and wiggled away with a laugh. "Wait. Darlene really did go to fetch me tea."

"Fuck the tea," he growled, lowering his head to hers again.

She set her fingers over his lips. "Let's just wait until she brings it in. Then we can tell her we're in a meeting."

He went still for a moment. "A meeting."

"You can say you're hiring me to plan another party. Do you have a birthday coming up?"

"No." His voice was a little curt, and he stepped away from her.

She frowned. "What's wrong?"

"I don't do backroom meetings, Adeline. I definitely don't want to do backroom hookups."

"This is your office. Hardly—"

"You know what I mean. You're ashamed of this."

She couldn't help the laugh that slipped out. "You think I'm ashamed of you? Mr. Perfect?"

He winced. "That's what you think of me?"

She reached out a hand with a teasing smile. "Well, you *are* Man of the Year. But what I'm thinking is I want to keep you all to myself—to keep this thing just between us."

He looked steadily down at her. "For how long?"

She sighed and squeezed her wet bun in agitation, trying to figure out how to make him understand, without letting him understand *everything*.

"I like you," she said quietly. "These past few nights have been . . ."

"Hot?"

She smiled. "*Definitely.* But I'm not looking for anything other than this."

"Hooking up, you mean."

"Come on," she pleaded. "You're going to be the *governor*. Eventually, you'll need someone who fits into that life. That's not me. It's never going to be me."

"I'm not governor yet."

"Okay," she said slowly. "So how do you see this going in the meantime?"

"I don't know," he said tiredly. "I guess I don't like that my own assistant and my closest friends can't know I'm dating someone."

"I know," she said quietly. "But you know how these things go. It starts with Darlene. And then the interns put two and two together and tell their friends. Or one of your bodyguards tells his wife, who tells her book club, and someone at book club knows a blogger, who knows a journalist. Before we know it, everyone knows that the mayor is sleeping with his event planner. It would be a disaster."

"For which one of us?"

"Both." *Your career, my heart.*

She looked at him, silently begging him to understand what she couldn't say. That a woman whose boobs were all over the internet, who'd once done nightly shots like the agave plant was going out of style, who *still* loved dancing all weeknight long did not a future Mrs. Davenport make.

He tensed his jaw, but she noticed he didn't contradict her. Instead he went tiredly back to his chair and sat down.

She came around to his side of the desk, her fingers brushing against his jaw, feeling it tighten beneath her palm, though he didn't pull away. Nor did he resist when she slowly lowered to his lap, her legs straddling his.

"I can leave if you want," she murmured, pressing her lips to the underside of his jaw, dragging kisses along the slight scratch of his afternoon stubble. "I don't have to tell you that I'm not wearing much of anything under this trench coat. I don't have to show you . . ."

His hands found her hips on a groan. "Adeline—"

Robert's desk phone rang.

His eyes darted to the side, then he reached out to hit a button, before glancing back at her. "It's Darlene."

"Answer it," she said gently, knowing and respecting that this was a part of his career, and that if he climbed the ranks like she suspected he would, it would only get more intense, more constant. And that there was no better man for the job.

He hesitated only a moment more before hitting a button. "Yeah." His tone made it clear that the interruption better be worthwhile.

Darlene's next words met that challenge and then some. "Mr. Mayor. The governor is here to see you."

Adeline went completely still, and completely cold, for reasons that had nothing to do with her damp clothes and wet hair.

The mayor's reaction was equally surprised. "How the hell was that not on my calendar?"

"I didn't know," Darlene said, sounding flustered. "Nobody told me, nobody called . . ."

Slowly, stiffened by shock, Adeline climbed off the mayor's lap, looking around.

"He says he needs to see you. Now," Darlene emphasized.

Robert dropped his head back against his chair, squeezing his eyes shut as he rubbed his forehead.

Adeline looked around the room in panic. She knew her father. She knew that in his mind, someone else's schedule was *never* as important as his. There was no chance he'd leave without seeing the mayor.

And there was no chance she could leave without seeing *him*.

She couldn't move. Didn't know where to move to.

Robert stood and gently grabbed her arm, trying to pull her toward the back of his office.

Her legs wouldn't work.

"Addie," he said sharply when she didn't move. "You can go out this way." He pointed to a discreet door she'd never bothered to notice before now. "It'll put you in a back hallway, and someone from my detail can point you to my private quarters."

She was flooded with relief and started to step forward when, all of a sudden, she realized he wasn't questioning her odd behavior. He was every bit as tense as she was. Both of which could be explained by him not wanting the governor to know he was entertaining in his private offices, and yet . . .

She stared at Robert. "You called me Addie."

He met her gaze steadily, and a dam seemed to break inside her head as more crucial details swept over her.

The fact that he'd picked her out of hundreds of event planners. The way he'd shown a personal interest in her from the very start, even urging her to share dark secrets. The unnecessary dropping by her office. The surprise on his face when she'd mentioned her mother.

And when she'd freaked out about him running for governor, he hadn't found her reaction unusual—hadn't questioned it at all. And just now, when she'd told him she'd never be First Lady of New York material, he definitely hadn't protested.

Because he *knew*. He knew she was Addie Brennan.

They continued to stare at each other.

"How long?" she finally asked.

He didn't pretend ignorance. "Always. Since the very beginning."

Her heart shattered, just as there was a persistent knock at his door. She flinched. "Please," she said, "I can't—I don't want to see him." Adeline wasn't sure she could stomach her father on her best of days, and this was far from that.

He nodded in understanding and opened the back door of his office. She slipped through, but he reached out and grabbed her hand. "Wait for me," he implored. "So we can talk."

She shook her head.

He squeezed her fingers, his eyes pleading. *"Please."*

Adeline wanted to tell him that he didn't deserve a chance to explain himself. He'd been lying this whole time, and he didn't deserve *her*.

It was the last realization that did it.

She'd been so focused on not being good enough for him, it had never dawned on her that she deserved the very best, too. She deserved honesty. Loyalty.

Answers.

Adeline pulled her hand away. "I'll wait."

Chapter Nineteen

Thursday, November 5

She didn't have to wait long. Or maybe she'd simply lost track of time, because it seemed only minutes before the mayor quietly opened the front door and stepped into the living room where Adeline sat.

His tense shoulders seemed to sag in relief when he saw her, though instead of coming to her, he dropped onto the couch across from where she was sitting, looking as exhausted as she felt.

Adeline broke the silence. "What did he want?"

"What he always wants. To bluster. Intimidate."

Adeline had noticed that Robert almost always erred on the side of political correctness. He rarely spoke bad of anyone, publicly or privately. That he seemed less than enamored with her father was a relief. She didn't think she could stomach it if they'd been cut of the same cloth, or even allies. He could be saying what he thought she wanted to hear, but Adeline didn't think so. The irritated disgust in his voice sounded genuine.

"He heard you were running against him?" she guessed.

"He's been angling for months to get me to admit it one way or the other. With the mayoral election behind us, I guess he thought he was owed an answer once and for all."

"Did you give him one?"

"I did. I told him he'd find out if and when I decided to make an official announcement. He thought he was due a courtesy. I said I'd start showing him courtesies when he started showing them to me, and showing up unannounced wasn't a strong start. He got pissed and left. The end."

"Does he know? About me? That I'm in New York with a new name, or that you and I are . . . connected?"

Robert shook his head. "No. Or at least he didn't mention it, and knowing him, if he knew, he would have." He leaned forward. "Okay, I've got to ask. How can he not know? How can he not know where his only daughter is—*who* his only daughter is?"

"I haven't spoken to him in years. And even before that, our exchanges weren't exactly what you'd call familial. But then, you already know that."

His gaze locked on hers. "I know what the media said. I also know firsthand the press doesn't always get it right."

She smiled a flat smile. "No, they got it exactly right. I doubt much of what you read was made up. Exaggerated, maybe. But the topless scandal, the partying, getting kicked out of boarding school . . . all true."

Adeline expected him to flinch, or at least look disappointed, but his expression never changed.

"What?" she challenged, when he didn't respond. "No questions?"

"I only want to know what you want to tell me."

Adeline snorted. "I can assure you that isn't much. There's plenty you didn't tell me."

"Plenty we didn't tell each other," he pointed out.

"Don't," she said, holding up a finger. "Don't sit there and act like you and I committed the same crime. Me not telling you about my crappy youth does not excuse you *using* me."

She expected him to deny it, but he merely nodded. "I know."

"Why?" she said, relieved that her voice was steady. "Actually, no, back up. How? How did you know who I was?"

"My campaign manager figured it out. It was his idea to get close to you."

She felt slightly nauseous at the confirmation that their entire relationship had been built on a lie from the very start. That she'd been so clueless. "To what end?"

Robert exhaled and sat back. "I need a drink. Want one?"

She wanted answers more, but figured maybe they'd go down easier with a cocktail. "Sure."

He poured them each a splash of whisky from the decanter on his sidebar, not bothering to put ice in either glass. He tossed the entire contents of one of the glasses back. He refilled it and then came back to Adeline, handed her the other glass, and sat.

"Your father's an asshole. I know it, my team knows it. There's been talk for years that he's not the esteemed gentlemen he presents himself to be, but we've never been able to get even a whisper of proof. The women, the drug use, the temper . . . all conjecture. Not a single person's ever stepped forward to confirm a single rumor on the record."

"And, what, you thought I'd be that person?"

"The bad blood between you and your father during the last election is no secret. The fact that you took a different name sort of confirmed you weren't exactly clamoring to align yourself with the man."

"No," she said curtly. "I am not. But I changed my name for a reason—to get as far away from that world as possible. Not *just* from my father, but from the girl I used to be. How could you possibly interpret that to mean I'd want to elaborate on the worst days of my life with a total stranger?"

"We didn't," Robert said. "Martin—I," he clarified, as though forcing himself to take accountability, "knew you wouldn't simply spill your guts to the mayor. But to a friend . . ."

She expected it, but the verbal blow still took her breath away. "Wow." She took a sip of the drink. "One of the oldest tricks in the book, and I didn't see it coming. Was sleeping together part of the plan, too, or just an unexpected bonus?"

"Addie." He broke off, looking frustrated. "Or Adeline—which do you prefer?"

"You don't get to call me either," she snapped. "Honey trapping, Mr. Mayor? Really?"

"Damn it. No! I was never intending to extort *you*, just—"

"Just take down my father by way of me."

He blew out a breath. "It was wrong. I knew it was wrong the second Martin brought it up, but he'd already scheduled that initial meeting with you. I swear to God, I was going to just politely send you on your way, none the wiser."

"Why didn't you? Why'd you have to—" She sucked in a breath and stood up, embarrassed by the memory of that first meeting and how much she'd *liked* him. "You know the worst part?" she asked, pacing around his living room. "When I showed up that first day, I was actually braced for this. I thought there's no way it could just be a coincidence that the mayor of New York would hire the daughter of the governor of New York. But you pulled it off. Like a fool, I left that meeting thinking I was just a really good event planner, and that you were none the wiser on my real name."

He stood as well. "You *are* a good event planner."

She whirled around, the tears she'd been successfully holding back stinging the corners of her eyes. "There are lots of good event planners. Why couldn't you have picked one of them? You said you were going to send me on my way, so why didn't you?"

Why couldn't you have just let me go?

"I meant to," he said, starting to reach for her, then letting his hands drop to his sides. "I did. But then you walked in, and . . . damn it, Adeline, I *liked* you. You intrigued the hell out of me the way I haven't been intrigued by a woman in a really long time. And I just . . . I liked being around you."

Adeline snorted. "Right. And if I just happened to tell you about my whole messy past and hand over details to destroy my father's campaign, then that was a convenient bonus to getting laid?"

"I'm not going to pretend I didn't want you to confide in me, but it stopped being for political reasons a long time ago. I swear to you, after I began to fall for you, I only ever wanted Adeline to confide in *me*, Robert. Not Addie Brennan to dump her secrets on the mayor."

After I began to fall for you . . .

Her heart leaped at the words, but she kept her brain focused on the realities of the situation. "That's just it," she said quietly. "Adeline Blake intrigued you. You took Adeline Blake to lunch. You hired Adeline Blake as your event planner. There's a whole other side to me that you don't know—"

"But I do," he interrupted, reaching out for her again. "I don't know exactly why you changed your name, and I won't ask. But you've been telling me these past few weeks that I don't know you, and I'd bet anything you've been terrified I'd vanish the moment I learned your real name. Am I right?"

Her lips parted as she realized he was right. She'd carefully protected her heart, thinking that Robert Davenport wouldn't come within a mile of her if he knew her real identity . . .

"I've known the whole time," he said, palms gliding up her arms, over her shoulders until he cupped her face. "I've known you're Addie Brennan. And I'm *still* here."

"If you know, then you must also know it would never work," she whispered. "The press, my father, the voters—"

"Aren't here," he finished for her, brushing his lips over hers. "It's just us, Adeline."

He pulled back, his gold eyes looking into hers, the air around them seeming to vibrate in anticipation of her response.

As she looked into his face, she realized that this was the first time she was seeing him as he truly was—not a mayor, not her father's political rival, not the enemy. Just a man who'd come to mean everything to her.

A man who was standing here wanting her—the good and the bad parts of her. A man who'd known her flaws the entire damn time and had never once walked away.

There had never been a web, she realized. He'd never been trying to catch her, to trap her.

He'd merely been waiting for her to trust him, thinking she was worth the wait.

And she was, she realized, letting the last of her insecurities slip away. She was worth the wait. She was worthy of this man, just as she was.

Her hands lifted to his chest, her fingers hooking into the lapel of his jacket as she pulled him closer. "Addie. My name is Addie."

Chapter Twenty

Robert's smile was the first seduction.

Slow and triumphant, it was the smile of a man who was about to devour something he'd been craving for years.

"Addie." Her name, said in a gravelly voice, was the second seduction.

He eased her to him, the expensive scent of him—leather and whisky and man—washing over her. The third seduction.

The fourth seduction took her breath away. Robert's hands lifted to her hair, fingers tugging out the pins of her bun, gently releasing the still-damp strands. He set the pins on a side table and ran his hands through her hair, seeming to relish the way the waves fell around her shoulders.

His head bent nearer. Lips hovering just above hers. Claiming. The fifth seduction.

His lips were firm and insistent, his tongue flirting with her bottom lip until she capitulated, opening to this man who had the power to hurt her, yes, but also the ability to make her feel the way nobody ever had.

Addie melted all the way into him, slipping her arms into the sides of his suit jacket, hugging him closer to her, taking comfort in his size. His strength. His warmth.

His lips trailed up to her ear as his hands slid downward, over her hips. "Are you really not wearing anything under this trench coat?"

She let out a surprised laugh. She'd forgotten about her seduction plan. He, apparently, had not. "Not *nothing*," she said teasingly, her hands slowly pulling his shirttail out of his pants.

His hands moved upward again, a little less steady now as they went for the knot of her coat.

She playfully pushed his hands aside. "Fair is fair, Mr. Mayor."

Slowly, deliberately, holding his gaze, Addie took her time undressing the mayor. She started with the suit jacket, easing it off his broad shoulders. Tossing it onto the back of the chair. She repeated the process with his tie, tugging the blue silk loose and hesitating only a moment before tossing it on top of the suit jacket.

"What?" he asked gruffly, noting her hesitation.

She smiled as her fingers went to his shirt and started undoing the buttons one by one. "Just thinking about all the interesting things we could do with that very conservative tie. Things that would make your constituents gasp."

"The only person I want gasping is you," he growled as she added his dress shirt to the pile of discarded clothes.

Robert reached for the belt of her trench once more, and again she pushed his hands away. "Uh-uh. We're not done here." She ran a hand over his chest, now covered only by the thin fabric of his white undershirt.

Narrowing his eyes, he reached behind his head and tugged off the T-shirt in one smooth motion.

Addie reached out again, an unintentional purring sound escaping her as her palm met the firm planes of his chest, the soft scrape of his chest hair.

This time it was her hands that were shoved away when she reached for her belt.

"My turn," he said.

She didn't move away when his hands found the knot of her coat, holding his gaze the entire time, even as the sides of the jacket fell open.

"You're beautiful," he said quietly.

Addie smiled in feminine pleasure that he appreciated her efforts, but her smile slipped when she realized he hadn't even looked down yet—he was still looking into her eyes when he said it. He thought she was beautiful. Not her body, not her lingerie, not her curves.

Her. All of her.

She hadn't realized how much she'd needed to hear it, to have someone *see* her, until this moment—until him.

His kisses were as sweet as his words, lingering and patient and tender.

Until they weren't.

He kissed her harder. Longer. His mouth growing hungrier, his tongue demanding everything from her until she finally arched into him with a pleading moan.

Please.

He touched her. Big hands on her waist, pulling her against him, his fingers exploring the shape of her rib cage, flirting with the edge of her bra.

Finally, he pulled back and looked down. His tortured groan was more than she'd hoped for. "Jesus, Addie."

His fingers stroked above the black lace, a low-cut balconette bra that covered her nipples, but just barely. The lace was lined with a pale pink ribbon that matched the bow of her thong. Something he found out when his rough hands shoved the trench coat off her shoulders, leaving it to pool around the black stilettos she kicked away.

He swallowed, the sound audible in the quiet room. "You're . . . you're . . ."

She lifted her eyebrows teasingly. "Yes?"

His eyes flicked up to hers. "Mine."

Now it was *him* who teased, bending down and dragging kisses across her chest, but avoiding her breasts, even as his hands roamed her stomach, butt, and thighs, whispers of touches that left her throbbing with the need for more.

Finally, Robert's hands closed over her breasts, seeming to revel in the feel of her, his lips pressing to the exposed swells.

His hands slid to her back, fingers finding the clasp of her bra. "Don't think I don't appreciate the way you look in this, but I need to taste you."

The bra fell to the floor, and Addie's back instinctively arched.

He gave her a wicked smile as he dragged his fingertip around her nipple. "Want something?"

She squeezed her eyes shut in frustration. "Please."

His finger drew closer to the tip, but denied her his touch. "Please, who?"

She opened her eyes and glared at him. "Please. *Robert.*"

He rewarded her by dragging the pad of his thumb over her nipple. His other hand lifted, repeating the motion on her left breast.

Over and over he flicked her nipples as her nails dug into his shoulder. He dipped his head. Flicked his tongue. Took her into his mouth and sucked until she was panting, the need between her thighs almost unbearable.

Robert's palm skimmed down her belly. Fingers slipped just beneath the elastic of her underwear, then back up over her stomach once more. He repeated the maddening circles several times until, finally, on a downward pass, he went lower.

Addie gasped as his fingers found her wetness. Moaned when he stayed there, his hand stroking and circling beneath the lace of her thong. She could have come like that—would have come against his fingers—had he kept touching her.

Instead he lowered to the floor, pulling down the sides of her underwear as he kneeled in front of her. He met her eyes at the exact moment his tongue touched her.

She cried out, her hands going to his hair, pulling him closer. Robert groaned his approval, his hand hooking behind her knee to ease her leg over his shoulder, opening her more fully to his exploring mouth.

His tongue slid over, bringing her to the edge with steady, rhythmic strokes, then backing away again to tease her with light flicks. She endured it as long as she could until her fingers grew desperate, tugging more insistently at his hair.

She felt him smile against her, a finger pressing to her opening, easing inside. He began licking her faster, and looking down at the mayor on his knees before her, Addie had a new realization about sex. It wasn't about the physical act. It was about sharing the moment with someone.

Then he pushed a second finger inside her, and all thoughts scattered as she gave in to a body-racking orgasm that would have sent her collapsing to the floor had his strong hands not held her up.

When it was over, she surprised herself by laughing, not in self-derision, not in humor, but in pure, unabashed joy.

He seemed to understand, because he was smiling as he stood, pressing a kiss to her collarbone. "Come to my bed."

"In a minute," she murmured with a smile. "Just one thing . . ."

This time it was her who dropped to her knees, dragging his trousers down his legs as he helped her along, kicking his shoes and socks aside.

She took her time peeling down his boxer briefs, teasing him with scattered kisses across his pelvis, her tongue accidentally-on-purpose brushing against him.

He let her tease. Up to a point.

Then he gathered her hair in his fist, guiding himself into her mouth.

Addie felt the moment his control started to fray at the edges. Felt it in the clench of his fingers in her hair, the thrust of his hips as he took her mouth. She opened her eyes, looking up his torso, and he let out an oath, pulling her off him and dragging her to her feet.

Naked, he bent to his pants and dug a condom out of his wallet.

"Since when have you carried that around?" she asked, as he tore it with his teeth.

"Since I met you." He rolled it on, and before she realized what was happening, he hoisted her up, pushing her against the wall, her legs draped over his hips.

He plunged into her, and she wrapped around him, welcoming the strong thrusts and harsh groans, the sounds of their lovemaking nearly as erotic as the sensations.

"Why can't I get enough of you?" he gasped, his face hot against her neck as he thrust faster. "I want—I need—Addie—"

Her name, uttered by this man as he was buried deep inside her, sent her careening toward the edge of another orgasm.

"Yes." His hands gripped her harder, his hips moving faster. "Come for me. Come with me . . ."

She did, her body clenching around his as he froze for a millisecond and then released inside her with a coarse groan, their hands and bodies clinging to each other, two parts of one whole.

Addie tipped her head back, resting it on the wall as she waited for her heart rate to slow. He set his forehead to her shoulder, his own breath still ragged, and she ran her fingers through his hair, now damp from sweat. He slowly let her slide down his body, until her feet touched the ground.

She braced for the unavoidable awkwardness that came from that sort of frantic, intimate coupling, but he merely stretched and grinned. "I like you looking like that."

"What, naked? Shocking. I'm sure you're the first man to prefer a woman without her clothes."

"Naked," he said. "With my mark on you." He reached out and pressed a thumb to a red spot on her shoulder. Then touched his fingers to her stubble-swollen mouth. "Sorry about that."

"Don't be." She pointed to the nail indentations on his biceps.

He glanced down, his smile pure, satisfied man. "You hungry?" he asked as he turned away, walking unabashedly to the bathroom to dispose of the condom.

"I—" She meant to say that she should go. That this couldn't happen again, that nobody could know about this, for both their sakes. Instead she found herself nodding when he returned. "A little. Yeah."

He bent to scoop up his clothes. "I've got some steaks in the freezer. Good?"

She smiled. "Great."

He started to head to the kitchen, then turned back. "Thank you. For thinking I was worth a second chance, even after I lied to you. Hurt you."

"We all deserve a second chance," she said softly.

Robert smiled, reaching out for her hand and lifting it, planting a lingering kiss in the center of her palm.

Addie's breath caught. *Tenderness.* The sixth and final seduction.

And the most dangerous of all.

Chapter Twenty-One

Monday, November 9

Robert and Kenny were drafting a polite *come back in January when the new guy's here* email. A lobbyist was angling to ban chicken wings in the city because of the choking hazard they posed for the city's domestic pets, and Robert figured it was the perfect welcome-to-the-job gift for his successor.

"'Best' or 'sincerely'?" Kenny asked, from where he typed the email to the chicken-wing guy.

"How about 'mild, medium, or extra hot'?" Robert muttered.

"'Sincerely' it is," Kenny said, just as Martin Tillman came ambling through Robert's office door.

"Hello, boys."

Robert nodded distractedly in greeting at his campaign manager, not stopping the pacing he did when thinking through what was next on his to-do list, then gave Martin a second look. He'd worked with the man long enough to recognize his I've-got-news grin.

"What?" Robert asked without preamble.

"Oh, nothing much. I just . . ." Martin took his sweet time sitting down, clearly relishing whatever juicy tidbit he was eager to share. "Did you know Charlie smokes?"

Robert shrugged. "So? He does it outside, away from the building."

"Oh, I'm not judging. I'm down from five a day to two a day, but I haven't kicked the habit, either. In fact, I got here early today and was making my way to the smokers' corner myself . . ."

Kenny, who'd been leaning over Robert's computer, mostly ignoring the conversation, stood up straight.

"Your boy here"—Martin pointed at Kenny—"was having a little chat with your lead security guy."

"They do that," Robert said, not bothering to hide his impatience. "Get to the point."

"Turns out, Charlie was wondering whether or not he should assign security detail to Adeline Blake," Martin said. "And I thought, why would an event planner need security detail?"

Kenny looked disgusted. "Eavesdropping, Tillman? You realize we're on the same team, right?"

"Are we?" Martin said, tilting his head to the side. "Because it sure feels like I'm the last one to know that the mayor clearly has a very personal relationship with the party planner if we're contemplating giving her a bodyguard."

Robert's stomach knotted. *Shit.* He should have known it'd be only a matter of time until Martin found out. For that matter, Martin should have been the first to know that he was involved with Addie so that the man could prepare a damage-control plan if the press found out.

The smarmy expression currently on Martin's face was exactly why Robert hadn't told him.

"Well done, Robbie. I didn't think you had it in you," Martin said with a gloating grin.

Robert's brain raced through options on how to handle the situation. *Deny? Divert? Distract?*

Deflect.

"Weren't you the one who told me just a couple weeks ago that I was an idiot to get seduced by her?" Robert asked.

Kenny jumped in. "He's right. In fact, I believe your exact words instructed me to 'make sure he doesn't go off the rails and get seduced by the one woman on the planet guaranteed to cost him the governor's seat.'"

"I'll admit to some lack of imagination," Martin said, sounding way too happy about his own shortsightedness. "But I'm on board now. I have to admit, I'm relieved to know you're willing to do what it takes to win."

Robert immediately shifted his strategy: *Downplay.*

"It isn't like that," he said quietly.

Martin laughed. "Sure, sure. A girl like that probably didn't take much sweet talk. She probably falls into any bed, with her legs spread."

Razor-sharp rage cut through Robert with so much force, he was surprised it didn't split him in two.

New plan: *Dismiss.*

"Get out."

Martin gave a disbelieving laugh. "What?"

"I want you to leave," Robert repeated.

Martin's laughter faded as he realized Robert was serious. "Oh, come on, man. You're the one who fucked her to get information. All I did was bring it up."

The anger cut even more deeply. "How can I be more clear? Get out of my office."

Martin heaved himself up, disgusted. "Jesus. Fine, go ahead and pretend you actually like the woman if that eases your conscience. Call me when you're ready to talk strategy—"

"I won't be calling you, Martin."

His campaign manager's smile was completely gone now. "What are you saying?"

Robert paused for a moment, giving the rational part of his brain a chance to overrule impulse and instinct.

Was he being hasty? Illogical?

But the rational part of his brain only confirmed what his gut already knew: he should have done this a long time ago.

"I'll always appreciate what you've done for my career," Robert said. "I'm grateful that you were a mentor for me in the early years. But I think we both know we don't see eye to eye anymore. I'd be happy to write a letter of recommendation—"

"Fuck you," Martin spat.

"Easy," Kenny murmured.

"Fuck you, too, Lamb," Martin said. "Don't think I don't know it was you who planted this idiotic idea in his head."

"Kenny doesn't have anything to do with this decision," Robert said. "It was my choice, based on your behavior."

"*My* behavior? Which has been what, getting you elected? Twice? For that matter, I've practically sealed a third election for you by dropping Addie Brennan in your lap. And now you're taking it out on me that you took the *lap* part literally?"

"I'm not going to change my mind on this," Robert said calmly, refusing to give the man any more ammunition on his relationship with Addie.

Martin glared at him a long moment, then gave a slow shake of his head. "Your father would never—"

"Stop," Robert said harshly. "My father hasn't been alive for over twenty years. We can't presuppose what he'd do in a given situation."

"*You* might not—you were just a kid. But I knew the politician that he was, and he would have done what was necessary—"

"He would have done what was *right*," Robert cut in. "I may not ever know what he'd do in my shoes, but I know what kind of person he was raising me to be. And it wasn't a man who'd use an innocent woman to advance his career. I'm ashamed I even considered it."

"Innocent woman, my ass. The whole damned country has seen her nipples. Maybe not as up close and personal as you have, but mark my words, Robbie, she'll be the end of your career if you let her. You know,

I'm actually glad I won't be associated with you when this goes to shit, and it will go to shit. I'll be on a beach somewhere with my severance."

"You'll get your severance," Robert said. "But forget what I said about the letter of recommendation. You won't be getting one from me."

"Fine," Martin said. "It'll save me from having to read your sanctimonious drivel." He turned toward the door, then turned back, his expression hostile but also sincere. "Let me give you one last bit of advice: You can have Addie Brennan, or you can be governor. But you can't have both."

Robert had no response for that. Even if he had, Martin was gone with an angry slam of the door, the slight tremor of the pictures on the office wall the only indication he'd ever been here.

"Well." Kenny exhaled. "That was . . ."

"A long time coming," Robert said tiredly, rubbing his hands over his face.

"I'd ask what took you so long, since the guy's a hell of a lot dirtier than you. But then, I guess that sort of proves my point. You're loyal."

"I *was* loyal," Robert clarified, feeling a twinge of guilt. "The guy's been there since the very beginning, stuck around after my dad died."

Kenny shook his head. "You said yourself that your father's been gone for years. You can't know what he'd do, or say, or think. Though, from everything I know of him, it might be safe to assume he wouldn't tolerate Martin's way of doing things now, either."

"I'd like to think not," Robert said. Then he shook his head. "Actually, you know what I'd like? I'd like to stop thinking about my life in terms of *what would my dad do*. I'd like to think for myself. To do what's right for me." He looked at Kenny. "Is that nuts?"

"No," Kenny said slowly. "But . . ."

Robert sighed. "Oh hell. Spit it out. I'm down an adviser, I need all you've got."

Kenny exhaled. "All right. First, I'll apologize for letting Martin overhear my conversation with Charlie. I had no idea anyone was within hearing range."

Robert shrugged this aside. "I know. In fairness to Martin, he actually had a point that he should have been one of the first to know that things between Addie and myself have grown . . . complicated." He paused. "What did you tell Charlie when he asked about providing her a bodyguard?"

"That I'd talk to you. I take it if he's asking, it means she's been . . . around?"

Robert gave a single nod. "She's stayed over. A couple of times."

Kenny blew out a breath, this exhale more apprehensive than the last. "You know what I'm going to say, right?"

Robert dropped into his chair, staring bleakly down at his thumbs. "That Martin was correct. About Addie."

Kenny took his time responding. "Not about her character. I've told you before, I like her. A lot. I even think, on a personal level, she's good for you."

Robert looked at the man he trusted above all others. "And on a professional level?"

"That's where Martin was right. I think you can have the woman. Or you can have the governor's seat. But you can't have both."

Chapter Twenty-Two

Thursday, November 12

"You know this is usually the scene where the unsuspecting woman *dies*, right?" Adeline whispered to Charlie.

"Well, you've got an advantage. Seeing as you *are* suspecting." The bodyguard gave her a brief smile over his shoulder.

"Not exactly reassuring," she said, quickening her pace to keep up with him as best she could in high heels fifty or so feet in the air. The railing was high and the floor felt secure, but she'd feel a lot better if she knew where she was going. She usually loved surprises, but not so much when they involved a catwalk.

Charlie halted, and she stopped as well, peering around him, both surprised and not surprised to see the mayor grinning at her.

She pointed at Robert, even as she addressed Charlie. "You're his *bodyguard*, Charlie. You had no issue with him wanting to hang out up here in the catwalk of a theater?"

"Oh, I had plenty of issues," Charlie said darkly.

"I thought you'd be happy," Robert said, his smile widening. "You don't have to worry about me getting shot up here."

"Right. Because nobody's ever been shot in a theater."

"Don't be macabre, man. Also, go away."

Charlie shook his head but did as he was told, disappearing from sight.

Adeline tilted her head as she looked in the direction Charlie had gone. "Maybe things have changed since I played the role of the governor's daughter, but isn't part of this whole bodyguard thing that he's supposed to, oh, I don't know . . . guard you?"

"There are only two ways up here," Robert said. "Both accessible by a narrow staircase. Charlie's at one, Roy's at the other. To say nothing of the rest of the detail milling around the entrances to the backstage area. Besides, nobody knows we're up here."

He emphasized his point by pulling her into a kiss, and Addie went willingly, even as a little part of her heart twisted in regret that they had to do things this way. Not that sneaking around didn't have its benefits. There was something undeniably sexy about forbidden trysts, secluded hallways, and stolen kisses. Plus, she'd been the one to insist on the secrecy.

But Robert was going along with it. Apparently, he'd decided he didn't mind the clandestine nature of their relationship after all. And even more damaging to her heart, he now seemed to *prefer* the sneaking around.

She'd thought it was what she wanted, and her brain did. Her brain knew that this was the way it had to be for *both* their sakes. The governor's scandalous daughter was never going to be the practical choice for a man with Robert's political aspirations. And the mayor was never going to be the right choice for someone with her political aversions.

Her heart, on the other hand—her pesky, stupid, falling-for-him heart—ached at the realization that this was all they would ever be. Sneaking around wasn't some short-term game; it wasn't them biding their time until they could go public with their relationship.

This was a *forever* kind of arrangement.

Correction: this was a *for as long as this thing—whatever it was— lasted* arrangement.

And realistically, she knew it wouldn't last long. It couldn't.

Eventually, Robert would need a woman who could be by his side at black-tie fund-raisers, who could travel with him on the campaign trail, who could make pretty speeches on his behalf, and have his perfect country club babies.

That wasn't Addie. It would *never* be Addie.

The prudent thing would be to call it now—the sooner she walked away, the less deep the cut, the less lasting the scars.

But Addie had never been prudent. She was more of the *life is short, have the cupcake* mentality. Robert was the cupcake. And she wanted him for as long as she could have him, whether that was two hours, two days, or two months.

She was hoping for the latter.

It was November, which meant he still had a couple of months before the new mayor would be sworn in and Robert could start campaigning in earnest for the governor's seat. At which point his relationship with her would be even more of an Achilles' heel than it was now.

Two months. And if two months was all she had, she'd take them and enjoy every damn second.

"Please don't tell me you brought me up here just to make out," she said, her voice hitching as his lips moved down her neck. "When I said I wasn't afraid of heights, I meant it, but I didn't exactly mean I relished them for no reason."

"Oh, there's a reason," he said, pressing one last kiss to her lips and then pulling back, nodding to the theater below.

As though on cue, instruments began their warm-up from the stage. "I know live events are sort of a no-go given our *not be seen in public* philosophy, but I had to figure out a way to take you to this."

"And *this* would be . . . ? There were no signs when we came in."

"There's usually not at these Julliard things. It's a student event, and they change just about every night. There is, however, a very classy paper program, made classier from having been shoved in my suit pocket."

He handed her a wrinkled program clearly printed on the cheapest paper available. She flipped it over so she could see the front cover.

THE MUSICAL CROSSINGS SERIES: MICHAEL JACKSON MEETS CLASSICAL

"You said you like exploring all kinds of music," he said, pointing to the word *Classical*. "But you also said you like Michael Jackson. Best of both worlds."

Addie didn't look up from the program.

"Hey." He nudged her leg with his knee. "We don't have to stay. If you're not feeling it, or if the seats suck, which—frankly, we don't have seats—"

"It's not that," she said. "It's just . . ." She looked up into his concerned hazel eyes. "You remembered. I mentioned that I liked Michael Jackson offhand weeks ago, well before we started sleeping together, and you remembered."

"Well, yeah," he said, giving her a confused smile, and leaning down. "See, that's what you do when you have a crush on a really cute girl. You learn everything you can about her so you can make her happy."

Happy didn't quite cover it. She felt something closer to infatuation. And not with the show. With *him*.

As though reading her thoughts, he gave a slow smile and moved closer. "You know, it just occurred to me. I think you had a hell of a crush on me, too."

She rolled her eyes. "Check your ego, please, Mr. Mayor."

"You did," he insisted with a grin. "I mentioned that I wanted my parties to be more fun. You made a mental note, remembered, and turned a black-tie event into a board game party."

"I made a mental note of your preferences, because you were *literally* paying me to make sure you were happy."

"And yet"—he kissed her mouth softly—"I'm not paying you now. But here you are, making me very happy. Like I said, hell of a crush."

She closed her eyes and kissed him back with every wonderful, awful, confused feeling in her heart. Hoping he couldn't sense the truth: she was teetering on the ledge of this being so much more than infatuation— something much more dangerous than a crush.

Chapter Twenty-Three

"So, there's something I've been dying to know," Robert said.

"Uh-huh. And it's something that had to be addressed during the workday? That couldn't wait until tonight?" Addie asked, leaning back in her desk chair and smiling into her cell phone. "For that matter, how do you have time for this call? I thought mayors of giant metropolises were supposed to be busy."

"I am. But I can't possibly even begin to process this proposal on increasing minimum wage until I know this. So, I'll never make a decision. And, well, I don't know, Blake, do you *really* want that sort of thing on your conscience?"

Addie rolled her eyes. "Fine. What is this nagging issue that I can help with?"

"Do you remember that late afternoon at my place? The one where we . . . got to know each other?"

Addie heated at the intimate memories. "There have been a couple afternoons like that recently. You'll have to be more specific."

"Well, one in particular comes to mind, when you looked like you had some very interesting ideas on what we could do with my tie. And I've been meaning to ask . . ."

"*Yesssssss?*" she said, drawing out the word with a smile, even though he couldn't see it over the phone.

"I want details. I want to hear every pornographic thought going through your head in excruciating detail. And then I want to act them out later exactly as they play out in your head. Much like we did last night with the . . . shall we say . . . props?"

"You know, I've been doing a lot of thinking," Addie said. "And I think the people of New York have a right to know their mayor has an extremely dirty mind—"

"Your fault. You've corrupted me. And you *like* my dirty mind. Don't deny it."

She bit her lip and smiled. She *did* like it. She liked everything about him. Too much.

Someone knocked at her office door, and she moved the cell phone away from her mouth so as not to shout in Robert's ear. "Yeah. Come in."

Cordelia opened the door and stuck her head in. "Sorry to interrupt. The mayor's chief of staff is here to see you."

"Kenny?" Addie asked, surprised.

"Kenny's there?" Robert asked, sounding even more surprised than she did.

"Yeah, you didn't send him?"

"No, I assumed he was just taking a long lunch."

"He says it's urgent," Cordelia said in a low, worried voice.

A tiny warning bell went off in Addie's head. She couldn't think of a single reason Kenny would be here on urgent business without the mayor's knowledge that would be good news.

The bell grew louder when he stepped into the doorway and she saw his somber expression. Nope. Whatever he was here to say was not good news.

"I'll call you back," she told Robert, ending the call before he could finish his protest. "Hey, Kenny, come in. What's up?" she asked, her nervousness making her voice sound borderline screechy even to her own ears.

"Hey, Adeline," Kenny said, glancing over his shoulder to ensure Cordelia had closed the door, and coming toward her.

Without preamble, he handed her an iPhone.

She should have been ready. Even before she met the mayor, she'd been mentally preparing for this moment, somehow knowing that it would happen, even if she didn't know the how or when.

Now, she wasn't sure knowing the how or when would have made a difference. She was pretty sure it would have taken her breath away, warning or no warning.

She looked down at the two photos of herself. One, taken years ago. Blonde and carefree, eyes shining bright with the joy of dancing, friendship, and yes, maybe a little tequila. The other taken mere weeks ago. A brunette version of her, with the same carefree happiness on the dance floor.

The dark hair that had served as a surprisingly effective disguise for the past year had failed her. Looking at the photos of herself side by side like this, blonde vs. brunette, there was no mistaking the fact that it was the same woman, just with different hair.

And in case anyone missed that fact, the headline below the images confirmed it:

Governor's Wild Daughter, Hiding in Plain Sight

Addie felt surprisingly calm as she read the article. It confirmed that Adeline Blake, event planner, was in fact Addie Brennan, wild child and national scandal from five years ago.

The author didn't claim to know where she'd been in between the last governor's election and her reappearance in Manhattan a year earlier, but it was extremely thorough in what she'd been up to since donning the Adeline Blake mantle.

The article went on to list her clients, including her most famous client, and the "unconfirmed rumors" about her having a relationship of a more personal nature with the mayor.

Then Addie's calm evaporated into a bone-cutting chill as she read the next line:

> While the mayor's office was not available for comment on Mayor Davenport's personal life, the governor had this to say about his estranged daughter's relationship:

> "A biological father doesn't get to choose his child. He can only do his best to reconcile himself to the fact that sometimes even the best parenting efforts go awry. On the other hand, a man does choose who to become involved with romantically, and all I can say is that a man who'd choose to get involved with a loose cannon like my daughter, well . . . I'm not sure that's anyone I'd want running my government."

"That son of a bitch," Adeline whispered quietly. "Best parenting efforts, my ass."

"I'm sorry," Kenny said, the genuine kindness in his tone easing the ache in her chest. Slightly.

She looked up. "The mayor doesn't know?"

Kenny shook his head. "I got a courtesy heads-up from an old college friend who works at the *Times*. They're planning to run it tomorrow, and I'll show Robert before then. But I thought you had the right to be the first to know."

"I appreciate that," she said quietly, staring down at the headline again before looking back up at Kenny. "This is bad, isn't it? For Robert's campaign."

He hesitated, and she sensed the usually straight-as-an-arrow Kenny had an out-of-character urge to lie to her.

Then he sighed and told her the truth. "Yeah. It's really bad."

Chapter Twenty-Four

Friday, November 20

Robert had just hung up the phone with his lawyer—his third call of the hour—when Addie stepped into his office.

At least he was pretty sure it was Addie.

He shot to his feet, barely registering Kenny quietly exiting the room, leaving the two of them alone.

Robert rounded the desk. "Where have you—I've been trying—What are you wearing?"

She peeled off the oversized sunglasses and wide-brimmed hat, then shrugged out of her coat. Not the sexy trench coat with very pleasant memories, but a huge wool thing.

"Disguise. Outside my apartment is crawling with paparazzi. Outside the mansion is even worse. I came in with one of the tours and waited until I could find Charlie to bring me through one of the back hallways. I don't think anyone saw me."

He wanted to tell her that it didn't matter. That he didn't care who knew she was here.

But of course, it did matter. And he should care.

Instead, all he could think about was the fact that it had been nearly twenty-four hours since their world had been turned upside down, and he hadn't been able to get ahold of her. Hadn't known if she was okay . . .

"What the hell, Addie?" he asked quietly, knowing the hurt in his voice came through, but not able to stop it. "Where have you been? I've called you a million times."

"I know." She tucked a strand of hair behind her ear, and he realized it was one of the few times he'd seen her out in public with her hair down. She looked younger. More like Addie from the gossip rags years ago, less like the buttoned-up Adeline. "I needed some time," she said.

"I get it," he said quietly, reaching for her, relieved when she didn't pull away. "I wanted to come by, but with all that's been going on . . ."

I couldn't be seen with you.

The thought made him nauseous, both the truth of it as well as the thought of her enduring her father's betrayal alone.

"I know," she whispered. "I understand."

His eyes squeezed shut. He *hated* that she understood. He hated that she thought she deserved to be hidden away and kept at arm's length like a pariah. He hated that if he had any other job, he'd have been able to laugh off her twentysomething antics. Hell, had he had any other job, he'd have probably had some twentysomething antics of his own that they could laugh about together, trading war stories of their wilder days.

Today, he'd woken up, wanting nothing more than to go to her; tell her to put on her tiny, sexy nurse costume; and then take her to a boozy lunch, maybe shoot the literal bird to any paparazzi.

Instead, he'd spent the entire day in meetings with Kenny and his team of advisers, trying to figure out his damage-control options. The verdict? There were no options. The overwhelming suggestion had been to put as much distance between himself and the governor's daughter and wait for it to blow over.

It had sucked to hear it then, but it sucked even more to see the expression on her face and know she agreed.

Robert felt a surge of resentment at the situation. He wouldn't lose her without a fight.

"All right, so I've got good news and bad news," he told her with a grim smile. "The good news is we're pretty sure it was Martin Tillman who leaked your identity to the press and your father, and we can press charges since he's in breach of contract. The bad news is—"

"We can't undo the damage he's already done," she finished for him.

He exhaled. "Yeah. That. Though, technically, it's still all conjecture. We can still try to—"

"Wait," she said, holding up a hand. "I know you have things to say, but . . . can I go first?"

"Of course," he said, trying not to panic at how distant she looked. He'd thought at first she was calm, and had been glad for it, but he saw now it was something else. There was a remoteness in her blue eyes that made his chest ache.

He tried to draw her even closer, but she pulled away completely, easing out of his embrace.

Robert sucked in a breath at the pain of the rejection.

"Would you . . . can you sit down?" she asked, her voice a little unsteady. "Over there?" She nodded toward his desk chair, and he realized with a sinking heart that she was distancing herself from him in every way.

"Sure," he managed, going back around his desk and sitting as requested.

Addie remained standing, first staring at her feet, then crossing her arms and looking into his eyes. "You've already probably figured out that the pieces surrounding Adeline Blake's mother and Addie Brennan's mother didn't add up."

He gave a slow nod. "I was under the impression your mother died in childbirth, and that your father raised you alone. Your mention of your mother's *recent* passing, and her inspiring you to be an event planner, admittedly caught me by surprise."

"I'd always believed the same story you did," she said in a monotone voice. "He even gave me a picture. A beautiful blonde with curly hair, a big smile, and bright eyes. She was the love of his life, and he'd been shattered when she'd died just hours after I was born."

She swallowed. "I believed him. Why wouldn't I? It was even on Wikipedia, for God's sake. But then, on my seventeenth birthday, just when he and I were really starting to butt heads, he fired one of his longtime bodyguards. A decent guy, who I think stuck around more for my sake than anything else. Jake passed me on his way out to his car his last day, and he's the one who told me my mother wasn't dead.

"I didn't want to believe him," she continued. "But the more I thought about it, the more it seemed like something my father would do. I confronted him, and he seemed almost smug when he told me that it was true—he paid her off to disappear and stay out of my life, in exchange for his promise that I'd receive the best of everything. But even after he confirmed she was alive, he wouldn't tell me where she was, her name, or even what she was like, and I just sort of lost it."

She gave a smile that held no joy. "That's about the time you started hearing about me in the news. A lot. I wanted to punish him, so I hit him right where I knew it would hurt the most—his reputation. I did everything I could to embarrass him. The drugs, the topless pictures, the guys, the partying. I figured if I pushed him hard enough, he'd give me her name."

Addie shrugged. "I learned the hard way that the more I tried to punish him, the more he punished me by withholding what I wanted most. The man is downright sadistic that way."

"But you found her," Robert said, his chest aching for the young girl who'd longed for something as simple as knowing her mother.

"Only because I changed my tack. Apparently, threats to *my* reputation he could weather. I think he even used it to his advantage to create sympathy—that poor, concerned dad with the slutty addict daughter.

But *his* misdeeds being presented to the public, on the other hand . . . those would be harder for him to overcome."

"You blackmailed him."

"Absolutely," she said, smiling without remorse. "You don't live with someone for eighteen years and not know what happens behind closed doors. I figured out *real* quick that the random women in our kitchen at two a.m. weren't 'just friends,' and that his weekend ski trips weren't with his buddies. The five-year-old girl playing hide-and-seek in her dad's office may not have known what that white powder locked in the safe was, but his fifteen-year-old daughter definitely did."

"Christ," he muttered, dimly realizing she was confirming everything he—and Martin—had suspected. That she knew her father's worst secrets. He was also surprised to realize that the only reason he cared right now was for her.

For the girl she'd been then, the woman she was now.

He took a deep breath. "What happened?"

"I offered him a trade. My mother's name in exchange for the flash drive with ten years' worth of photos of him with other men's wives. Evidence of his cocaine habit. The time he punched out the gardener for getting his new BMW wet. He accepted the terms, and we agreed never to see each other ever again."

Addie smiled, a real one this time, even though her expression was distant. "Mom was a brunette, as it turned out. Not blonde. Straight hair, not curly. But other than that, she was everything I wanted her to be. Everything my father wasn't. Kind and loving and generous."

"I'm sorry you lost her."

"Me too," she said lightly. "But those couple years with her in New Mexico, she was more of a parent to me than he'd been in the decades I'd lived with him. I had what I wanted most. Someone to love me."

His eyes watered, and he cleared his throat. "I'm so sorry, Addie. About what a bastard your father is. About your mother. About the fact that I even thought of using your past for my own gain."

"But you didn't," she said. "You wouldn't. I think I knew that all along. It's why I let myself trust you. You're a good guy, Robert."

Maybe. But I'm sure as hell not a courageous one.

"About the story that broke yesterday," he said, desperate to make things okay so he could keep her near. "We can deny it. They don't have any proof. We'll be extra careful for a few months, and then—"

"I don't want to deny it."

"Yes, and then—" He broke off when her words registered. "What?"

Her gaze was sympathetic, a little sad, but determined. "I'm done hiding who I am. I'm done dyeing my hair and feeling ashamed of my past. I didn't do anything wrong, not really. I certainly didn't do anything unforgivable. I'm through letting my need to distance myself from *him* also mean I distance myself from *me*. I *am* Addie Brennan. You've known that all along, but I don't think you really know what it means. I like dancing and late nights. I like dirty jokes and dirty sex, and though I'll admit to some regrets about my past decisions, I can't undo them. I don't think I *would* undo them.

"But I'm *always* going to be the woman with that past. Even if I could overcome past scandals, I don't want a life where I'm terrified to make a single wrong step and end up on the front page. I just want to be me, and I think we both know that I'm not what the Davenport legacy needs."

Damn her for saying that last part. For forcing his brain to deny his heart what it wanted. For forcing him to choose between honoring his father's memory, being a respected leader, and the woman who'd stolen his heart.

He stood and braced both hands on the desk, looking at her. *Pleading* with her. "I don't want to lose you, Addie. I don't know what to do, but I know I don't want to lose you."

She gave a sad smile and stepped toward the desk, setting her palm to his face, stroking her fingers over his cheek in a gesture that felt devastatingly like goodbye.

"Robert. Can you look me in the eye and tell me that being with me—in public, for real, for everyone to see—can you tell me that won't hurt your career? That being the guy who slept with his opponent's loose-moraled daughter won't cost you the governor's seat and any other elected position?"

He wanted to deny it. He wanted so badly to scream from the rooftop that it wasn't true, that they could weather anything.

But there were rules to public life. Rules to *his* life.

He dropped his head in defeat. "No. No, I can't say that."

"And can you tell me that it doesn't matter? That it wouldn't hurt you to give that up?"

He squeezed his eyes shut, unable to look at her. "No." He said it in a harsh voice.

"I know," she whispered, leaning down and brushing her lips over his cheek.

He opened his eyes, just in time to see her hand setting something on the desk between his splayed palms. He stared at the small thumb drive. "What's this?"

"You already know," she said with a smile, stepping back. "It's the reason you hired me in the first place. Everything you need to bring down Governor Brennan. Pictures, a couple videos, a written statement from my mother, the falsified death certificate."

His head snapped up. "I stopped wanting this a long time ago." *After I fell for you.*

"So do it for me," she said, moving toward the door. "You're going to make a hell of a governor, Mr. Mayor. And I can promise you'll have at least one vote from the Manhattan district."

"I don't want your damn vote, Addie. I want . . . *you*."

She was already gone.

Chapter Twenty-Five

Sunday, November 22

"Have I mentioned how good it is to have you back?" Jane said around an enormous bite of her French toast.

"Only . . . I don't know, what has it been, ten times now?" Addie asked, glancing over at Rosalie.

"At least ten," her friend confirmed. "But to give her a little credit, she's totally right."

Addie picked up her mimosa. "You two act like I've been dead for the past few years." Neither friend said anything, and she put the glass back on the table with an exasperated look. "Oh, come on. It hasn't been that bad."

"No," Jane was quick to reassure her. "But I've got to admit, there was nothing quite so satisfying as helping you pack up all those blazers for the Goodwill."

"I don't know," Rosalie said, helping herself to a strawberry off Jane's plate. "Going with her to that hair appointment was pretty great, too."

"Not for me," Addie grumbled. "Nobody warned me that going from dark brunette to blonde was going to be a hell of a lot harder than going from blonde to brunette. I sat in that chair for nearly four hours."

"But it was worth it," Jane said. "Right?"

Addie touched the honey-blonde knot at the back of her head and smiled. "I feel like myself again, so yeah, I'd say it was worth it."

"Okay, okay, show her," Jane said, tapping excitedly at the table in front of Rosalie. "You brought them, right?"

"Brought what?" Addie asked suspiciously as Rosalie leaned down and picked up her purse.

She dug around until she came up with a small white box wrapped in a red ribbon, which she placed in front of Addie. "For you. From us."

"I feel like I should point out that it's not my birthday, and that you shouldn't have, but I can't deny that I freaking love presents," Addie said, tugging off the ribbon and lifting the lid off the box.

"Business cards?" she asked in confusion, seeing the neat, even row of cards. She fished one out and read the front.

Her eyes watered immediately. "You guys."

"Cordelia helped us order them," Jane said. "We wanted them to match your current Jet Set business cards with the logo, but with a little change."

A very crucial change. She ran a finger over the name printed in tidy black font: Addie Blake.

"You said you wanted to find a way to blend Adeline Blake and Addie Brennan," Rosalie said softly. "You're already partially there. You kept Adeline's hair style but went back to Addie's color. You kept Adeline's company, but went back to Addie's fashion sense."

"And this way," Jane said, reaching out and tapping the corner of the card with her finger, "you can still be Addie *and* ditch your disgusting father's last name."

"I love it," she said with a sniffle, tucking the card back into the box and reaching out to squeeze both of their hands across the brunch table.

"Are you sure? Because we can keep calling you Adeline—"

"Addie," she said firmly. "Adeline's fine, but it's a little formal. Addie is, well . . . me."

"You're not worried someone will put the pieces together?" Jane asked. "With your blonde hair you look pretty much exactly like your old self."

"Yeah, do you not age?" Rosalie asked with an exaggerated pout. "Even your boobs look like they're stuck in a time warp. How are they so perky this close to thirty?"

"I think they're just happy to be out of the blazers," Jane said. "Like flowers, finally able to reach for the sunshine."

"You're making me regret this dress," Addie said, looking down at the maroon wrap dress that hid enough to be classy, but revealed enough of her hourglass figure to make her feel like her old self.

She hadn't realized just how badly she'd been locked inside herself until the truth about her identity was out in the open. She'd thought being exposed would be her worse nightmare, but she realized now that hiding had been the real nightmare.

Now, it was as though Adeline and Addie finally had made peace with each other, and she could simply be who she was instead of who she used to be, or who she was aspiring to be.

She was Addie Blake.

A blonde who preferred buns. A businesswoman who preferred bright dresses to black blazers. A woman who contributed to her 401(k) and went dancing on weeknights.

She finally felt whole again.

Well, except for the mayor-sized hole in her heart, but she was working on that day by day.

"The dress is fabulous," Rosalie reassured her, then took a deep breath. "The eyes, on the other hand . . ."

"What's wrong with my eyes? Is my makeup smeared?" She lifted her hands to check her mascara.

"They're dead," Jane said bluntly. "As in, you look dead behind the eyes because you broke up with the mayor."

"Jane," Rosalie chided.

Her friend shrugged. "I'm just saying. She hasn't talked about him. That can't be healthy."

"There's really not much to talk about," Addie said lightly, taking a sip of her drink. "It doesn't matter what color my hair is, or what I call myself—someone like me is never going to fit into his world. Even if I could bury my past, I don't want to. I'm done hiding who I've been and who I am, which means I'd only ever be a liability to him."

"How do you know?" Jane protested.

Addie gave a pained smile. "Because I asked him. And he let me walk away."

She'd hoped that saying it aloud would help her come to grips with the way things had ended, but as she confided in her friends, she felt the ache in her chest squeeze tighter than ever before. Somehow, she'd stupidly thought that knowing the end was coming would make it easier. But over the past couple of days, she'd realized that while she'd been mentally prepared for the fact that she had no future with Robert Davenport, she hadn't been emotionally prepared.

Her brain had been braced for it. Her heart had been straight up blindsided.

"Please tell me you fired his ass as a client," Rosalie said.

Addie shook her head. "I didn't have to. He doesn't have any party needs, and when he does, I'm sure Jada will be back. End of story."

"Just one more question," Jane pleaded. "Then we can drop it."

"Fine. What?" Addie relented with a sigh.

"Does he know you love him?"

Addie flinched. She'd refused to let herself even touch on the *l*-word. Somehow, she knew the second she let herself acknowledge that she loved him was the moment she'd break apart.

Her friends exchanged a look at her lack of response that she pretended not to see. She understood their concern, but she also knew there was no solution for this situation other than for her and Robert both to move on. The sooner the better.

"I can't," she said quietly. "I *can't*, so can we please talk about something else?" She turned toward Rosalie. "Have you found a new job yet?"

"Or a new apartment?" Jane said after a pause, a good enough friend to know when to drop a subject. "Whoever owns that Airbnb you're staying in was way too fond of discount seafood."

"That's true," Addie agreed. "Last time I was in there, it smelled like a very suspicious fish market."

"Yeah, that happens when the air freshener runs out," Rosalie admitted. "But I think I'm close, both on the apartment and the job front. I've got a final interview this week, but no talking about it. I don't want to jinx anything or psych myself out."

"Fair enough. Can we at least toast?" Addie said, lifting her glass. "To new beginnings. Jane just got a promotion, you're on the verge of a new home and a new job, I've got new hair and a new name . . ."

"Well, sort of your *old* hair and your *old* name," Jane said, pragmatic as ever.

"Just be quiet and lift your glass," Rosalie said.

Jane did as she was told, and the three women toasted to fresh starts, new beginnings, and making peace with old demons.

She'd let go of her baggage. She'd let go of her father, who'd never really been much of a father at all.

Now, if only her damn heart could let go of a certain mayor . . .

Chapter Twenty-Six

Friday, December 4

"Mr. Mayor?"

Robert jerked slightly in his chair, glancing across the table at his new campaign manager. "Sorry, what was that?"

Rosalie Fabre gave him a smile that was both patient and annoyingly *knowing*. The price he paid for hiring Addie's best friend as his new campaign manager, he supposed.

But he didn't regret it. Though it had taken no small amount of convincing to get Rosalie to come on board, she was the blast of fresh air the team had needed. She was the exact opposite of Martin. Her ideas were modern and innovative instead of Reagan-era, her mannerisms cheerful and upbeat, her strategies straightforward and aboveboard.

He didn't exactly enjoy that he couldn't look at her without thinking about Addie, but that would ease with time.

Probably.

Maybe.

He wasn't counting on it.

"I was asking if next weekend worked for you to make the formal announcement for your bid for governor," she said. "I really think the timing is as good as it's going to get. Bashing his own daughter—and you—in that article backfired on Brennan. His approval ratings are as low as they've been in two years, and he's been digging himself in a hole by continuing to bash you at every turn. Something that you're spotlighting by refusing to play. He's looking increasingly like the surly old-timer throwing dirt when someone else's back is turned."

"The younger generation in particular is loving your strategy to play completely clean," one of the interns blurted out.

Robert thought about the flash drive sitting locked in his safe. He wished he could say it was the easiest decision of his life, opting not to use the content on it. Not because he'd wanted to beat the man in a stupid election, but because he'd wanted to make the man pay for the way he'd treated his daughter. And if the governor came after Addie in any way, Robert wouldn't hesitate to send the contents directly to every news outlet in the country.

But for now, it was a last resort. After firing Martin Tillman for his underhanded tactics, Robert didn't want to be a hypocrite. He also couldn't be sure that, for all Addie's insistence that she wanted him to use the intel, he could do so without hurting her. He couldn't highlight George Brennan's sins without bringing his daughter into the spotlight, and Robert wouldn't do that when he knew Addie needed to put her father behind her.

Robert had also been thinking a lot about *his* father lately. Without Martin there to chant in his ear about the Davenport legacy every other meeting, Robert had been starting to remember things differently— more clearly.

He'd remembered his father as a respected man of influence, yes, but he also remembered him as a dad. A husband. He'd remembered that his dad had never cared if Robert and his friends had been noisy when he'd been on the phone, or gotten mad if streaks from Robert's afternoon brownie got on his white shirt when Robert had hugged him after work.

When Robert had come home from baseball practice bragging about his triple, or proudly shown off his first-place spelling bee certificate, his dad had always said, "High five! Did you have fun?"

The memory was both bittersweet and jarring. *Did you have fun?* How many times in Robert's adult life had he asked himself that? Ever?

And lately, Robert had been wondering something else, something even more treacherous to his future: In his quest to carry on his father's legacy, had he ever really stopped to think if his father would even *want* this for him? Robert Sr. would have been proud. He was sure of that. But he was beginning to suspect that his father might have been a little disappointed as well.

Disappointed that his only son had chosen a perfect image over an imperfect *life*.

Disappointed that his only son was making decisions based on a man long dead, instead of a man *alive*. Most disappointed, perhaps, that Robert wasn't living for himself.

That he wasn't really living at all.

He'd spent nearly every waking minute of the past two weeks, including in meetings like this one, trying to define what he wanted out of his life.

But no matter how many times he pictured his perfect life, he realized it wasn't perfect at all. It was wonderfully imperfect. Messy. Surprising. Exhilarating.

Perhaps most importantly, he'd realized that it was never about *what* he wanted.

It was about *whom*.

He sat up straight and cleared his throat, fixing his attention on Kenny and Rosalie. "Set up the press conference. But I want to change up a few things . . ."

Chapter Twenty-Seven

Friday, December 11

Addie shook her head as she tightened the blue ribbon wrapped around the vase holding a bouquet of red and white tulips. She hissed in irritation when she realized her hands were a little shaky.

She gave them a subtle shake, glancing around the room to make sure nobody noticed the event planner was downright jittery.

Would she never learn?

Nearly three months ago, she'd stepped into the mayor of New York's web because of a party. Today, she was doing the exact same thing.

Well, not the exact same thing. Back then, it had been curiosity that had her showing up at his office. Today, there was a _little_ bit of curiosity, a _little_ bit of doing Rosalie a last-minute favor as a friend . . .

And _a lot_ of something else.

Today's event was smaller than the black-tie event at Gracie Mansion back in October. Which, in theory, should have made it easier. She'd been responsible only for basic decorations and coordinating a caterer.

A job, quite frankly, she could have—and should have—off-loaded to one of the junior event planners. But she'd wanted to be here. Not for the event itself, which she could do in her sleep. But because the reason for today's event was important to Robert.

As of this evening, he would officially be announcing his candidacy for governor. And as painful as she knew it would be, a final nail in the coffin of their would-never-be relationship, she wanted to share in it, even from a distance.

And distance was definitely what she'd been after. Rosalie had even guaranteed she wouldn't have to face him if she didn't want to, that she could stay in the kitchen and watch the mayor's speech on TV.

But Addie had already decided she needed to see him in person, even if it was just her blending in with the crowd. She just wanted to know that he was okay, that he wasn't as gaunt as he'd seemed on TV these past couple of weeks, that the shadows under his eyes had been her imagination or bad lighting.

Addie heard a crackle at the side of her head and lifted her hand to adjust the earpiece.

"Addie?" Rosalie's voice said in her ear.

"Yup, here!"

"How are we looking?"

"All good on my end. The tables are set, the champagne is chilling, the spotlights have been tested and retested to make sure they'll highlight Rob—the mayor—without blinding him, and the pizza is scheduled to be delivered within the last five minutes of his speech. So long as he doesn't run over, it should be hot."

"You're *sure* on the pizza?" Rosalie asked. "I trust you, but this is a political campaign, not a first grader's Batman birthday party."

Addie smiled a private smile. "I'm sure." *Italian sausage and mushrooms.*

"All right. I guess you know your parties," Rosalie muttered.

She did. She also knew Robert.

Addie couldn't help it. Her eyes scanned the slowly growing crowd, knowing he would still be in the backstage of the hotel's conference area prepping his speech, but her heart craving a glimpse of him all the same.

As expected, there were plenty of men in suits, but none of them six foot two with warm hazel eyes and a smile that could turn her inside out.

"Okay, looks like we are a go on all fronts," Rosalie said. "Oh my God, do I sound like a control freak? I know this isn't usually the campaign manager's job to coordinate like this, but it's my first event, and—"

"You're doing fine," Addie said. "It's like I told you. You were born for this job."

She'd been surprised when Rosalie had told her about Robert's job offer, but pleased. He couldn't ask for a better campaign manager than über-efficient, innovative Rosalie, and Addie had reassured Rosalie that she knew Robert to be a fair and kind boss.

The lights began to dim, save for the ones onstage, and Addie was surprised to realize how much the crowd had grown since she'd last paid attention.

They'd forgone chairs, since Rosalie had indicated the speech would be short and sweet, and the standing format would allow the event to transition almost immediately to a celebratory cocktail vibe.

Better for Addie. Much easier to blend into the crowd during his speech, then disappear to the back during the party.

She wondered if Robert knew she was at the event. Knowing how control-freak he could be about these things, he *must* know, and he must have okayed Rosalie hiring her.

But he hadn't gotten in touch. Not even a simple well-this-is-awkward text.

It stung more than it should. She'd been the one to walk out, but still, it had been torture not hearing a single word from him, not knowing what he was thinking or what he'd decided to do with the intel on her father.

Not knowing if he was seeing anyone else . . .

The painful thought faded as Frank Sinatra's "New York, New York" began playing over the speakers, the way most of the mayor's events had begun in a charming, if slightly teasing, way.

She'd thought she was prepared, but the second he stepped onstage, Addie felt like she couldn't breathe.

She'd missed him. *She'd missed him so much.*

Oblivious to her turmoil, clueless to her presence, Robert strode across the stage, waving at the crowd with a wide, confident smile on his face, nodding in acknowledgment of the cheers.

"Thank you," he said, adjusting the microphone at the podium slightly, with the ease of someone who'd spent a lifetime speaking to the public. "Thank you. Thank you. Thank—Okay, settle down."

The crowd laughed, then quieted.

"If I need to introduce myself, you're probably in the wrong room, but for posterity's sake, for the guy in the back with the video camera, I'm Robert Davenport, and for the past eight years, I've served as mayor of New York City."

The crowd cheered again, and he waited with a smile for it to fade out.

"I've spent a lot of time over the past few months wondering what happens for me after January. After I turn over the reins of this city I love so much to the capable hands of Ned Olivo. After I walk out of Gracie Mansion for the last time, not as the mayor, but as a resident. I suspect everyone in this room, most everyone in this *city*, assumes I'm here today to announce what's next—to announce my bid for the governor's seat. And up until a few days ago, I actually thought that myself."

Wait, what?

Addie blinked in shock, and the crowd began to murmur quietly in anticipation that a twist was coming.

"It's always been the plan," Robert continued. "Mayor. Then governor. Maybe a brief stint as an Avenger, if Marvel ever calls me back."

The crowd laughed but was no less on edge, the media's microphones leaning forward with even more urgency now, as though desperate to hear it first and break whatever news awaited.

"I thought it's what I wanted," he said, "and it's a job I still have great respect for. But it's not a job I want any longer. Not at this time."

He stood silently a moment, his head bowing just briefly, hands braced on the podium. When he lifted it, his eyes were clear, his voice confident. "Many of you have heard rumors about my personal life in recent weeks. This surprised some of you, no doubt because some of you thought I didn't *have* a personal life."

A few chuckles, but mostly the crowd stayed silent. Rapt. None more so than Addie, her hand over her pounding heart.

"And the truth is, I didn't," he continued. "I've dedicated every last second of each day, every ounce of my being, to this job. To being the best mayor I can be. To serving this city the best way I know how. I'm proud to say that while I've certainly never pleased everyone, my tenure has been relatively free of controversy. This has been intentional on my part. Every decision I've made has been with the intention to do the right thing. The virtuous thing. I expect it's why I escaped the recent rumors about me dating Governor Brennan's daughter mostly unscathed. I was allowed the mistake because it was my first one. Most of you in the press have all declared it already behind me. Forgiven. A tiny blight on a perfect record."

Addie gasped as she registered that he was talking about her. In public. On camera. She barely noticed people were starting to look her way. And look again.

A reporter turned and took her picture, which in turn caused a dozen more people to glance her way, but Robert continued, unaware of the scene he was causing.

"But here's what I've come to tell you today, ladies and gentlemen: I don't care how that 'mistake' affects my political career, because I don't believe it *was* a mistake. And I've realized I want something more than a perfect record."

Robert shifted then. Just the slightest turn to his right, but his eyes found hers immediately, and Addie realized he wasn't oblivious at all. He'd known she was here the entire time, right down to the precise spot where she was standing.

He held her gaze as he spoke. "I won't be defending my relationship with Adeline Blake, because it needs no defending. I won't be discussing how much I care about her, because that's nobody's business but mine and hers. What I can tell you is that, for the foreseeable future, I'll be taking a step back from politics to focus on my personal life. I believe in voters. I believe in government. I believe I can do some real good in this world, and I intend to do exactly that."

Addie's hand went to her throat as his gaze seemed to grow warmer the longer he looked at her, the crowd seeming to disappear.

"But I also believe," Robert continued, "that in order to be the best leader I can be, I need to be the best *man* I can be. And I can't do that alone. I don't want to do that alone. My life's about to get messy, my reputation might pick up a few blemishes. I've been thinking a lot about my late father, who taught me plenty of things, and whose exacting standards I've always aspired to meet. But my father was one of the good ones."

He turned again, this time to look directly into one of the cameras in what Addie knew was a pointed message to George Brennan.

"My father was one of the good ones," Robert repeated. "And I know he'd be the first to tell me that there are more important things in life than reputation. That it's more important to be a good person than a manufactured paragon of perfection. My father was a great man, but what I remember most about him is that my father *loved*. And he was loved. *That's* the legacy I'm choosing to live on his behalf."

Robert cleared his throat, looking down at the podium a moment before lifting his head to look at the crowd. "I hope to serve the exemplary people of this city again someday." His gaze came back to Addie's. "In the meantime, I'll be working on being the type of man you deserve. If you'll have me."

She wiped at the corners of her eyes, knowing that he was talking to her. Only her.

"Thank you, and good night," Robert said quietly, stepping back from the podium.

For a moment, there was only deafening silence. Then the entire room seemed to erupt, the front row of the press manic to be the first to get a question in, even as heads began turning to stare at her, the fact that the infamous Addie Brennan was in the house having circulated through the room like wildfire.

"Addie?" Rosalie said in her left ear. "Can you hear me?"

Addie jumped, having forgotten her earpiece. She pressed a finger to her ear and tried to back out of the pressing crowd, away from the noise. "I'm here."

"If you want to get out of here, say the word. I promised the mayor that I'd get you here, but I made him promise that if you wanted to leave, he had to let you. Just say the word. Luciana is already here to help with the party."

"What'd she say?" a muffled male voice said into the earpiece.

"Mr. Mayor. Respectfully, please hush," Rosalie said to the voice.

Robert.

Addie went to her toes, trying to see the stage over the crowd, realizing that Robert was no longer addressing the reporters but was off to the side of the stage, talking to Rosalie, who Addie could just see through the curtains.

"What'd she say?" Addie heard him say again, more agitated this time.

Addie let out a startled laugh. "Oh my God, Rosalie, *that's* why you have the earpiece?"

"It's not Rosalie."

Addie froze as Robert slowly turned to face her across the room, something that she assumed to be Rosalie's earpiece held up to his face.

"Hey," he said softly, when their gazes collided.

"Hey," she managed.

"Rosalie made me promise I couldn't turn you into a spectacle unless you wanted to be."

"A little late for that," she said, giving an obvious glance to her left and right and the dozens of people who were very aware of what was happening between her and the mayor.

He grinned across the room. "What can I say? I met this woman who's made me rethink the appeal of a scandal."

"Oh, this isn't a scandal," she said. "This is small-time. They'll forget about it by next week."

"Huh," he said, his eyes seeming to warm her, even across the room. "Any interest in giving them something to gossip about for years?"

She could have sworn he was holding his breath, waiting for her answer, but she couldn't be sure. Her own heart was pounding too loudly, as though it wanted to burst right out of her chest in happiness.

"Addie?"

"Ah, what the hell," she said with a watery smile. "Let's give them something to talk about."

His smile seemed to freeze for a moment, as though he were afraid he'd heard her wrong. And then it grew very, very wide.

She watched across the room as he handed the earpiece back to a beaming Rosalie. He strode purposefully across the stage. Down the steps.

The crowd parted for him, the entire room now apparently aware, or at least suspecting, what was happening, and everyone wanted a front-row seat.

Addie didn't care. She barely noticed.

And then he was in front of her, his gaze unabashedly adoring and not caring who knew it.

"Good speech," she said nonchalantly.

"I thought so," Robert said, stepping closer. "You have a favorite part?"

"Hmm." She pretended to think it over. "You said something about Addie Brennan. And how much you cared about her?"

"Did I?" he asked. "I must have messed that part up. What I meant to say was how much I *love* Addie *Blake*."

Her eyes filled with tears. "See, now *that* would have been a great speech."

"Allow me a redo, then," he said, bending his head to hers, his lips pressed against her ear, his pronouncement for her only. "I love you."

"Robert." Her chest tightened in bittersweet happiness. "I don't want you to give anything up for me."

"I'm not giving up anything. I'm *gaining* everything. Assuming, of course, there's any chance you could love me back? Someday?"

She looked into his eyes and saw the raw emotion and honesty of a man who did everything wholeheartedly. Including, apparently, loving her.

The tightness in her chest loosened, a warm feeling wrapping around her as she realized how much she'd longed for this ever since her mother died.

Someone to love her.

"Addie?" He touched her cheek. "Do you think . . ." He cleared his throat. "Is there any chance . . ."

"That I could love you?" She pretended to check her fingernails nonchalantly, and he narrowed his eyes. "Maybe someday . . ."

"It better be someday soon. Otherwise I'll have to marry you so I have every single day to try to convince you to love me back."

"You convinced me," she whispered. "You convinced me a long time ago."

His eyes shone down into hers. "Yeah?"

"I really do love you," she whispered, just before he lowered his mouth to hers.

It was the sort of kiss for which there were no words, no way to describe the perfection of that moment when you realized you'd found someone to spend your life with.

"We've gone and done it now," she said with a laugh, when they finally pulled back for air, flashbulbs going off all around them. "They'll be talking about us forever."

"Good," he said, pulling her in once more. "Because that's exactly how long I'll love you."

Epilogue

One year later

A New Era in New York Politics

Yesterday marked a change in the guard in New York politics. In a startling upset, Alicia Rivera, a relative newcomer who quickly became a household name after being backed by last year's Man of the Year Robert Davenport, defeated incumbent Governor Brennan in a landslide victory.

As for the former mayor himself, who shook up the political scene earlier this year by announcing a bid for a Senate seat instead of heading for the governor's mansion as long predicted, Davenport celebrated his victory in New York City last night alongside his new campaign manager and longtime chief of staff, and with his new wife, Mrs. Addie Blake Davenport, by his side.

AUTHOR'S NOTE

Thanks so much for reading *Yours in Scandal*!

This story is one that's been a long time coming, and one that's actually a culmination of ideas. I've known for years that I wanted to write a story about a politician who falls for his opponent's daughter. I've also loved the idea of exploring what it would be like for someone to be unexpectedly thrust into the national spotlight by being named a magazine's Man of the Year, in the same vein as *People*'s Sexiest Man Alive.

Let's just say it was a pretty great moment when the muse nudged me in the direction of *combining* those concepts. The second that inspiration struck, Addie and Robert's book became clear in my mind: a man who everyone sees as "perfect," and a woman who's been labeled with all the nonsense that our society sometimes can put upon women.

I always enjoy writing love stories, but I will say that Addie and Robert's romance was extra rewarding. I may be biased, but I'm not sure two characters have ever deserved happily-ever-after as much as these two, and I hope you feel the same!

Be sure to sign up for my newsletter to stay up-to-date on the next Man of the Year story about a hotshot baseball player who heads home for his high school reunion, only to find the high school sweetheart he left behind isn't quite so easy to leave a second time . . .

PS: Looking for something to read in the meantime? Check out my website for my entire backlist! If you loved this one, I think you may also enjoy *Runaway Groom* and my 21 Wall Street series.

ACKNOWLEDGMENTS

Excuse me for a moment while I roll out the red carpet for . . . *drumroll, please*

My amazing editor, Kristi Yanta.

We've worked together on more than twenty books now (I can't even believe that as I'm typing it!), and while I'm always so grateful to have her in my camp, I think with this book, perhaps more than any other, she deserves the biggest medal / trophy / glass of wine in the world.

Kristi, thank you for not flinching even a little bit when I handed you my tattered first draft and a plea to help fix it up into the love story I knew it could be. Your patience with the process, as well as your uncanny sense of knowing exactly where the plot and characters needed to go, helped turn this one from a pile of words into a book I'm supremely proud of. No pressure, but you must never, ever leave me.

To the fabulous team at Amazon Publishing, I'm so delighted to have a place on your roster. Thank you for all you've done to make the Man of the Year series a reality, especially my editor, Maria Gomez, for always giving me creative freedom and championing my writing, and the fabulous marketing and author relations team for helping spread the word about my books. Shout-out to the behind-the-scenes team, the production coordinators, the copyeditor, the proofreader, and the fabulous cover designer—you guys are amazing!

To my "squad": I'd be nowhere without you. To my agent, Nicole Resciniti: thanks for never rolling your eyes (*right?!*) when I text you at five a.m. with yet another idea. To my assistant, Lisa Filipe, for taking on all of the *stuff* so that I can spend as much time as possible in my writing cave. And speaking of my writing cave, there are very few people allowed in, but Jessica Lemmon, Rachel Van Dyken, and Jennifer Probst, there will always be a chair and a cup of tea with your name on it. *Not.* There will always be a chair and a glass of wine with your name on it.

To my husband, Anth, who just handed me a plate of scrambled eggs as I was writing this. Thanks for never complaining about just how many meals I eat hunched over the laptop, and for always being the best thing about my life when I close that laptop.

To all of my readers: I'm so grateful for you. Thank you for your kindness and your love of romance.

ABOUT THE AUTHOR

Photo © 2019 Anthony LeDonne

Lauren Layne is the *New York Times* and *USA Today* bestselling author of more than two dozen novels, including *Hot Asset, Hard Sell,* and *Huge Deal* in her 21 Wall Street series, as well as her Central Park Pact series. Her books have sold more than a million copies in nine languages. Lauren's work has been featured in *Publishers Weekly, Glamour,* the *Wall Street Journal,* and *Inside Edition.* She is based in New York City. For the latest updates, be sure to check out her website at www.laurenlayne.com.